THE REVENGE OF THE FOXES

THE REVENGE OF THE FOXES

by Ak Welsapar

Translated from the Russian by Richard Govett

Edited by John Amor

Cover and interior layout by Max Mendor

Cover image used under license from Shutterstock.com

ISBN: 978-1-912894-10-9

Published: 31.10.2018

A catalogue record for this book is available from the British Library.

AK WELSAPAR

THE REVENGE OF THE FOXES

TRANSLATED FROM THE RUSSIAN BY RICHARD GOVETT

GLAGOSLAV PUBLICATIONS

CONTENTS

In my heart I never lie.

Sergei Yesenin

LOVE FOR LIFE

In Neskuchny Gardens the glow of the birch and aspen trees was quietly dying. Moskva River, densely filled with yellow leaves, was softly singing its autumn song. All around there reigned a silence, nourished by the rain and the moisture under the earth; it rested on the leaves which were falling from the tall trees of the gardens, on their rises and descents leading away from the noisy avenue, from the endless stream of cars near the river bank, which at this weary pre-evening hour was somehow deliberately deserted. In this silence the conception of the future springtime seemed to be taking place; this was the sunset of the Great Day, which every year begins with the noisy springtime break-up of the ice.

"Will this autumn be my last?" I thought, sitting almost at the very edge of the water. "And will I die suddenly?"

Now, several years from the day when I was completely immersed in one question – life or death, I can see still more clearly how close was the abyss… which, to my great happiness, did not engulf me. And today my spirit aches for those young lives broken off in very take-off, for those friends of mine, for whom the rivers of springtime will no longer start to rumble as they break the ice, for whom everything is stilled for all eternity in a deep winter sleep.

* * *

I remember that autumn, I remember the vicissitudes of time and the departing warmth, I remember the feeling of pain. Each leaf of the old oak tree in the hospital courtyard would break off and fall, as if counting the minutes; longing and grief filled my spirit. The doomed autumn leaves would try with their last strength to break out of their predestined circle and save themselves from extinction. They hastened in flocks after chance passers-by, alarmed by the movement of their steps. Caught up from the moist earth by a gust of wind, the leaves would cling to people and tag along with them like stray dogs, ready faithfully to serve anyone not driving them away like noisome flies. But no-one would stop, they all passed by and, deceived in their treasured hopes, the yellow and red leaves would fall into the mud and long continue to flutter in an attempt to rise and rush after new passers-by.

I had plenty of time to observe the metamorphoses of that autumn, so unrepeatable for me; there was nowhere to hurry... a pity, there were few distractions, and all the ones that we had were thought up by me, by us, just slightly to brighten up our miserable hospital life. I remember we terribly enjoyed being strikingly different from the other patients wandering like the ghost of Hamlet's Father in plain, boring, colourless clothes, whom we met during the so-called 'short walks'. And we others, not wearing official gowns, were allowed to wear our own clothes! We walking wounded heart patients were in principle healthy people. And it was difficult not to strut our home wardrobe, thanks to which, hardly outside the field of vision of the strict nurses, (albeit for a short time, but with relish) we cast off the 'label' of invalid, and it was like becoming normal people like those flowing in the endless stream along the pavement of the huge avenue in front of the Institute of Cardiovascular Surgery. Sometimes we managed to melt in with this crowd, indifferent to everything and ever rushing somewhere, and go on desperate walks. Of course, this was done at great risk: you could not fall under the gaze of the doctors or the medical personnel – no one wanted to be written off before the operation for 'non-observance of the regimen'. Although our Institute was not one of nuclear, but human research, the regimen operating in it was no slacker, incidentally, than any place where Soviet (strict) rules and daily routine were in force for inter-institutions. Nevertheless we managed not only to cross the avenue and buy 'Pepsi' or 'Fanta' in the shop, but also go on long walks and travel on the Metro as far as the Lenin Hills and from the heights there cast a glance at the busy transient world which one of us might soon have to leave forever...

Who was to embark on a journey into such a distance depended on many factors, including the boldness of the patient, and on how he found himself in the Institution where at public expense (that is, almost gratis) the person was having his life returned to him. Whether he got into the Institute from a faraway peripheral hospital – a hotbed of flies and insanitary conditions, after a long queue of those waiting to go under the knife, or whether they brought him here without red tape, backstairs by '*blat*', by the standard bribe. Of great importance also was the status occupied by his patron in the institutional hierarchy and consequently the status of the patient himself.

But enough of that. I am now occupied by something else: the fearlessness of the heart patients who, not of their own will, found themselves facing the choice "to be or not to be". Trusting the surgeons with their hearts, they firmly decided – TO BE!

∗ ∗ ∗

When they led me to the doors of the ward, I glanced at the sign – No.6... Immediately there floated into my memory the name of the classic which 'glorified' the number of the ward of sad fame, yes... a fine start, it augers nothing joyful for me, but we will hope that the ill-omened number will not be fateful for me; anyway, the writer was telling the world a story about lunatics and not heart cases.

"Vitya... Slava... Akhliman..." I was introduced to my ward neighbours by Olga Nikanorovna, the Ward Sister for children with innate heart defects. "They are good children and great fun!"

"What fun!" I thought as I looked around the ward and met the eternally sad eyes of Vitali. "Just try and laugh it off!"

"I am going now and you take your places!" the Sister said smiling, in a tone which might be appropriate in a café or a bar but not here among people awaiting a risky heart operation. "Here is your linen and everything else," added the girl handing me the sheets. "Babka Nastya said she would make the beds so wait, maybe..."

"No matter, I'm used to it."

"Take care..."

With the departure of the young Sister it became even more melancholy in the ward. Having briefly given my name, I somehow bungled the moment of acquaintance and hurried outside, unable to bear the pressure of three pairs of eyes scrutinising me. Perhaps I'll feel better outside the walls of the ward.

The garden was lovely but just as miserable: I wished for nothing, I foresaw nothing good, I dreamed of nothing. All around autumn reigned, leaves were falling, there was the odd passer-by, not far away the avenue hummed, and in the midst of all this was I, but what of that? So melancholy, it was enough to make you sob! My nearest and dearest were so far away that it was better not to think about them. In an attempt to drive away this monstrous thought, I looked helplessly around me: there were people as miserable as I. Under the old oak tree sat a threesome, men in grey overalls. They had probably huddled together to jointly drive out their sadness and longing… I wondered where I should go, to the avenue or to those people as yet totally unknown to me. I had just decided to approach them (I would anyway have to get to know them sooner or later – they were coming down from our floor, as I was going up with Sister Olga) but I was prevented by a middle-aged woman.

"Anatoli Yakovlevich…! Tolya…!" her voice rang out and one of the men quickly jumped up from the bench.

"Manya…! My Masha has come!" his mouth immediately stretched into a smile.

I decided not to make their acquaintance and quietly went away. I wandered a little in solitude, and not being able to think of anything of use, decided to return to the ward.

"What a miserable institution, eh?" I muttered, standing with my back to the Memorial to Bakulev.

My words, not addressed to anyone in particular, were heard, and this is what is strange! An answer followed.

"Here they operate on the heart of the Motherland!" pronounced a sickly thin young girl in a simple dress, standing at the doors of the Institute.

"And has She a defect?"

"Yes," she replied with a barely noticeable nod.

"Specify," I said, continuing my 'interview'. "Is Hers innate as well?"

"Judge for yourself," she said, looking at me with a frown. "It's obviously not acquired so it needs radical intervention, surgical moreover. In any case that is how it seems to me…" she added.

"Excuse me, young girl, but how old are you?" I looked into her big, slightly bulging, thoughtfully sad eyes, extremely surprised at her sophisticated talk.

"What, is it of such interest?" she made a sickly face.

"Well," I shrugged. "It is of course interesting for… I have to know what to give you: flowers or sweeties"

"Impudent!" she was offended and left.

This conversation left in my spirit something not very pleasant, unclarified, uncertain. I seemed to have offended this young girl – fine, if she is really still a teenager, then, like a child, she will sulk for a bit and then forgive the unintended insult. I did not have long to wait for clarification. When, after a walk, I went down into the basement to the changing room, the young Sister Olga Nikanorovna met me with a curious look.

"What are you doing, Nazarli, offending our girls?" In her question I could not help hearing a frank challenge. I had no means of objecting, so I restricted myself to a response with an indiscriminate: "Have I really offended someone?"

No doubt the Sister took my question as a veiled attempt to object. Not unsurprisingly, she did not delay with a thorough reply and gave me a direct moral lesson:

"If you consider 18-year-olds to be children and 25-year-olds to be grannies, then, of course, all is in order! Does that not embarrass you?" she elicited, looking at me with either a teaching or a corrupting look from under her thickly painted long eyelashes. Her eyes wavered deceivingly between absolute seriousness and mystery. "Is that not offensive, eh?" she drew out each word theatrically reproaching me, whilst at the same time arranging something in the cupboard. "Or where you come from in the Karakums – is that the practice?"

"No! It is not the practice," I quickly responded, upholding the right to the high cultural standards of the people of my native desert. "I simply did not recognise the adult in her, and she, as it turns out, has already managed to tell tales on me?"

"That sums it up… you need to be careful when dealing with women," the Sister advised me quite sincerely, surprisingly mildly and with a certain tenderness.

"I will try," I replied with a smile, almost at a loss.

"We will be checking…"

And she did check: our relationship began to develop with extraordinary storminess. Only a day later we locked ourselves in that same changing room, hid from everyone, and especially from Babka Nastya, and kissed passionately, like actual lovers.

"The greatest danger here is Babka Nastya!" Olya warned me immediately between kisses. "Kissing here is forbidden, meaning it is not welcomed, and Babka Nastya has taken upon herself the role of voluntary inspector. She is trying to eradicate love in the Institute and considers that it is superfluous here…"

The girl told me this breathlessly, abruptly, descending more and more to a heated whisper, which made our kisses hotter and more desired, because – may Babka Nastya know this! everything forbidden and persecuted is much sweeter than what is permitted. That Olga was right I soon convinced myself. Babka Nastya persecuted loving couples as the Inquisition did heretics. "It's not done here!" she would shout for all the Institute to hear, the louder, the nearer it was to night time. The trouble was, Babka Nastya herself, to all appearances, was no small a sinner in her youth, and could with one glimpse calculate with mathematical precision who was looking especially in whose direction and who was not indifferent to whom. This is how she whipped up our illicit love with swinging blows, not allowing it to burn out within the tedious walls of the Institute of Cardiovascular Surgery.

"Baba Nastya, you should go home," we would tell her nearer to night time. "What are you, the watchman? What do they pay you for? You are Matron, your time finishes at 1800 hours!" She would not go. She chased us everywhere and shamed us. "Baba Nastya," we would tell her. "Don't chase everyone, you haven't the strength for it! The future belongs to us if, of course, we live to see it…" But no, she would not agree! "Go home, Baba Nastya," we would tell her. "Tomorrow you have to get up early, you have to go round the wards and check that they've all gone to sleep in their own beds!" But she would not leave her post. She would mumble that the Metro was closing early, that it did not operate round the clock or maybe till five in the morning. Evidently, at home no-one was waiting for her, or she had no-one to order about. And so, she lived at the Institute.

Did Babka Nastya understand our feelings? Did she realize that for many of us sick people each day was like the last, the very last in our lives? We were not being unfaithful to our lovers, nor were the girls being unfaithful to theirs. We were not betraying anyone, we were only trying to cheat fate. We young men and women heart cases saw in our chosen girls and boys a source of Life, from which we had to drink deep before embarking on a perilous voyage poised over a dark abyss…

"Against all Babka Nastya's knavish tricks," I would tell my dear Ward Sister Olga, "you and I have one claim: we want to love! To love each other desperately, and this requires of me to love and of you a sea of tenderness to captivate the soul! For you are, perhaps, my last love on this sinful earth." And I thought to myself that I might never come to see the mother of my child, she is so far away and my life may be broken off at any minute. "Olga, Olenka, they say women cannot really love, they are only capable of pitying a man, so pity me as the peasant girl pitied the brigand at large, whose time was up, and is now being led blindfold to the branched oak. Have pity on me as the storm pities the ocean, as the Heavens pity the Earth!"

In reply she held me tighter as if hiding me from the coming danger.

"I shall pity you, my sweet: I shall torment you as the storm torments the ocean! If only your little heart would hold out, everything will be alright with me, I seem to have been waiting all my life for you, I'm in love!"

"Tell me," I continued, inspired by her reply. "Tell me, my precious, can I call you my very own? My Olga…"

"Nikanorovna, you mean?" she queried, for a moment breaking off her kisses, which had quickly become grown-up ones.

"Yes," I replied, "Olga (my) Nikanorovna!"

"You can call me Dish, only don't put me in the oven!" she joked.

"Are you married?" I continued to ask her between ardent kisses.

"No longer!" she replied with a sigh.

"Ah, no longer? Don't fret, I swear I never dreamt of better, in our time this is more of a merit than a shortcoming, it means you're free…" She smiled ironically. I hastened to explain:

"I swear to God that divorce beautifies a woman and imbues her with living fire. You know, you belong to the better portion of tender creatures by whom I have been educated, taught to kiss. How delightful that we have hidden from everyone! I am yours, only yours, allow me to love you so that there awakens in me a wild thirst for life, so that I believe – I was born to love you and you me! Ah, Olya, Olga (my) Nikanorovna, I do not know if I have much time left in the world. Oh, I do not know… my heart is racing like an unbroken horse, at full speed, it is striving to the secret peaks of happiness, to the unknown, it wants if only a little longer to love in this world… we will not lose the precious moments, time is running through our fingers. You say, wait till night, when they are all asleep. Ah, have we enough time to wait? Daylight is no bar to love, do not be fastidious! Incidentally, as I see it, you touch-me-not, Olga (my) Nikaronovna, by God, did you always sleep with your husband in an overcoat? Why do you tremble so tenderly? Your body and breasts are resilience itself, your lips are barely opened pistachios of Badkhiz! How did you and your husband spend the winter Moscow nights together in bed? What did your husband expect from this life, apart from you? A fleeting, transient, illusory life!"

My over-sensitive Ward Sister only kept silence, she was at this moment incapable of pronouncing even a single coherent sentence, she burned like a candle in the dark changing room, carried away by our suddenly kindled passion. Soon our brief ardent meetings in the changing room became regular.

"You understand," I informed Olga (my) Nikanorovna, when we had once more managed to hide from everyone, and especially from Babka Nastya, who was scouring the far corners seeking out precisely us. "You understand, my final love. A meeting can be arranged or contrived but you cannot invent parting. This dream will end in an operation, blood, mortal anguish – you must know that not everyone returns from there alive..."

"You're talking nonsense..." she whispered.

"I agree," I replied. "Do not expect from me any profound insights in the changing room when there are only a few days left to the heart operation. I am at the mercy of life and thirst for love is my only living space. Let whoever wishes to, condemn me afterwards, but not now. Now there is nothing for me but love, for love is the supreme manifestation of life! There is nothing higher than love in this life and never can be. That is how life is created."

"Lord," The young Ward Sister whispered, trembling in soundless sobs. "How cruel is Fate, how cruel she is..."

"Don't cry! You are now crying not for me but for yourself, because you often see those who stand on the margin between life and death. It is not known to whom this path is allotted, in the final count we will all sooner or later meet there... but better love me now than afterwards. Consider me already grass in the meadow, a tree on the roadside, a drop of the sea fallen from heaven! If I am not to survive the dangerous trial, if I am destined to leave for my forebears so early – so be it. Perhaps I am grieving in vain, seeking in this life a temporary refuge, grasping at you, as at a straw? And if I am really to live on, then let life itself make this known to me, let it fight for itself. And if nevertheless I am not to survive... I will take with me into the darkness which awaits me, the warmth of your hands, the taste of your lips, the tremor of your body... I know you are my last love in this life."

"No," she quickly replied with surprising calm. "People like you fall in love often. I will not have time to blink an eye and you will be in the arms of someone else, you just see..." She suddenly looked at me with a soft reproach as if anticipating the events which, as she thought, must inevitably occur, all this in tears.

Now I embraced the girl still tighter, and stroked her shoulders, and she trustingly reposed in my embrace; barely waiting, she soundlessly brushed away her unsought tears. We were silent, each thinking our own thoughts.

How I want to live! Perhaps I will still be given time to enjoy the first rays of the sun at dawn, to delight in the quiet melody of the leaves, the sound of the waterfall, the twittering of the steppeland birds of a spring morning... how I want to live...

* * *

Any of the seriously ill who could fully adapt to the Institute with its strong smells ingrained in the walls, its sub-standard sanitation, could be strictly counted among the strongest living beings in the world. Unfortunately, to the great distress of the medical personnel and the patients, the Institute obviously lacked the finance for capital maintenance, and so all the incredible efforts of the nurses and matrons were reduced to nothing, so what was the point of scrubbing the unpainted floor for years on end, if plaster was going to fall on it continually from the ceiling? Ah, if only someone from the yawning government heights would pay attention to the pitiable state of the Institute, flout the restrictions of the five-year-plan and help with funds?

But people will not get used to these outrages, they will just become reconciled and force themselves to submit to the circumstances, because only the person himself can compel himself to suffer anything, and no brute can do that for him. At the Institute people saved themselves in different ways: some, the older ones, who had lived with an innate defect till their grey hairs, would pray, while others, the younger ones, would watch them and secretly, no doubt, they believed that in a neighbourly way some of that grace, which could be obtained by prayer, would be transferred to them. We, the young ones, found consolation in what the older ones could no longer and were not even resolved to find: we would fall in love. Love gave us freedom, it liberated us from the difficulties we experienced every minute. None of us wanted to finally admit that death was a reality. We both admitted it and did not admit it. We did not wish to feel like sick people, but willy-nilly we had to. We were continually tormented between two fires. This was so obvious that it was slightly irritating every time I was picked from the flock of my peers and taken immediately for some sort of routine examination: I would have tests, be listened to, tapped, radiated with various rays penetrating the human body with ultrasonic waves.

"You've done those tests on me already!" I would say indignantly. "And X-rays too! Sounding? No, we haven't had what we haven't got. Ashkhabad hasn't got that, so it's so far not possible. Why is the equipment not there? The equipment is there, it was bought in the last five-year-plan, but there is no-one to operate it. The specialists will be trained in the next five-year-plan. Yes, everything to plan! How should I know where they plan? In Moscow, probably!"

"When did you arrive?" Barygin, head of department, asks me. He is so full of the sense of his own greatness that he notices nothing around and straight ahead of him. (To everyone's luck, this arrogant peacock was not to work at the Institute for long, he would soon be removed for certain violations.)

"A week ago, Semyon Semyonovich," I reply. "I have a question for you... Can I transfer to a different ward? Which one? Practically any so long as the *fortochka* ventilation window opens, but in our ward it is jammed, there is no fresh air and it smells. I find it stuffy and suffocating. Yes, I can? Thank you! What? Re-register? (That means first book out, then book into the queue for the operation, with the same complaints, naturally... then wait a year or two...) I see, a mere trifle, just a formality! I will make use of it at the first opportunity, but not now, of course, as I'm already here."

But success unexpectedly smiled on me! I was allowed to change ward without re-registering, because I was suddenly required in another ward. Under orders from that same Barygin, Babka Nastya told me to follow her.

"Babka Nastya, where am I to 'follow' you? To another ward? But surely Barygin said I couldn't?"

Here the old woman taunted me:

"It's that you couldn't jump from ward to ward, love, like a grasshopper. But to ensure the appropriate living conditions for a foreigner – that's another matter, for this the regulations can even be broken. You are now going to be my translator, you see!"

"Ah, for the foreigner in number eleven, the Greek? Yes, I saw him in the corridor, nice lad, a mixture of masculine and refined beauty. No wonder our lady heart specialists are already starting to go out of their minds! But how am I to be translator? I don't know Greek! In English? But suppose he doesn't want that, after all, he's Greek and not…"

"We'll manage," says Babka Nastya, hurrying me along. "He knows English."

"He knows it? You've talked to him, have you?"

"He's got an Englishist look, dear."

"Ah, you guessed from the expression on his face! But what if it's a Greek expression and not an English one?"

"Come on, don't ask so many questions! Why should a Greek speak Greekish? Abroad there they speak international, that's English!"

"Truly, iron logic, I give up! Who speaks his native language now? Damn it, how didn't I come to think of that?"

My flow of questions only dried up at the doors to what was to be my new ward. I had obviously dealt Babka enough questions, the way she grunted at me, putting a warning finger to her lips, as if to say speak sense to him and not idle rubbish!

* * *

"Hello!" I say to the tall, handsome young Greek, whose Achilles Heel is the interventricular septum, as if his mother, bathing in the sacred waters of the Styx, held him by his tender little heart. The heart eventually did turn out to be unprotected, and this ailment brought Apostolis to Moscow.

"Hello!" he replies, seated in the accustomed pose of the fast grower, slightly bent in a pose which he adopted as a teenager, when he suddenly found himself taller than all his classmates, and was obliged, when interacting with them, to bend slightly, as if feeling to blame towards his friends for having shot up so. His aquiline nose supports a forehead without a bridge. His face is noble and fresh, and if you met the lad by chance in the street, you would never think he was a heart case. Incidentally, I was never taken for a sick person, I was always considered healthy. But the danger accumulated from year to year, like senile fatigue, and I suffered worse and worse from colds. That is the way with the ailment.

Apostolis was glad to have someone to talk to. He pronounced the words softly but with an unfailing "r", which is a fault among almost everyone who learns English without a real teacher.

"How many days ago did you undergo surgery?"

"Five."

"Nice, and you're already up? Don't get up, lay down!"

"It's nothing, I can do it…"

"Do you need something?"

"Thank you, but I need nothing."

"If you need something, just tell me…"

"Well, thank you!"

Just then, everyone who felt like it burst into the ward and the first, of course, was Lida. After her came Vitya and Sergey and then Valya.

"But where's Akhliman?" I asked.

"Gone walkabout," Lida drawled with a plaintive voice.

An enchanting blonde with shoulder-length hair and a direct, open look (Mary, as she introduced herself) sat in a corner and silently looked around our two-bed ward, whose inhabitants seemed to her more like princes of the blood than ordinary patients. Her quiet silver tones I heard right at the end, when she said, addressing everyone, but primarily Lida:

"Let's go, folks, they're probably tired…"

After congratulations on my moving in, my friends went their own ways, and I took pleasure in the cleanliness and comfort of the new ward. Everything here was so clean, the sheets were gleaming white, the heavy, rusty old beds had for all their worth tried to give themselves a delicate new lease of life so as not to betray their pitiable condition to the overseas guest. But the people, the staff of the Institute, tried even harder…

Before sleep, Apostolis and I talked about Dostoevsky. The young Greek was convinced that Dostoevsky was a prophet, a saint, who long before the October Revolution foretold what socialism could turn out to be for Russia.

"No," I contended. "Dostoevsky does not even pass for an ordinary theoretician."

"What?" Apostolis was taken by surprise. "Dostoevsky is a prophet and a genius!"

"Maybe," I tried to pacify my neighbour. "Maybe he is a prophet and a genius, but few heard him. They built socialism here after his *Devils* and, as you can see, nothing came of it. That is, something came, but not what they expected, a great deal of blood was spilt. Far better to build it after Marx, blood might have been spilt, but rather less, not a sea.

"Yes," he replied with disappointment, and made a look of tedium. Such tedium that even in the morning I saw an unpleasant trace of our conversation on his face. Why he felt so keenly for our socialism, I was to find out later.

And so, in the morning and after breakfast, before the arrival of Lida, a woman of about thirty, sharp in both words and movements, I was in a better mood than Apostolis and was even jokey. But Lida came. And the expression on her face, unusually gloomy and irritable, took me aback. "What's shaken you up, Lida?" my look inquired.

"Why are you jumping the queue?" she said malevolently, with a sideways glance at my neighbour.

"He doesn't understand anything, speak more clearly," I requested. "What are you on about?"

"Why are you being operated on out of turn? I got a bed before you! And so did Valya and Anatoli Yakovlevich! How does it turn out like that? Who fixed it for you? Jamalov, was it?"

In the back of my head, somewhere deep under my skull, I felt the twitch of something hitherto unknown to me, a vein or – I don't know – a little blood vessel, fine and small, but malignant.

"Where did you get that from? I don't know anyone at the Institute. How have you decided it's Jamalov? I haven't asked him. And anyhow, he's not my fellow countryman. I'm a Turkmen and he's an Azerbaijani. But when are they taking me for the operation?"

"On Monday. The timetable's already been put up, you can look for yourself."

"Fine!"

"But how did you arrange it?" Lida persisted.

"I argued with the foreigner!" I teased. "That way they'll cut without any queue. If you like, you say a couple of nice words to Apostolis and you'll go under the knife next week. They're sure to operate on you then, that's what our country's like! Don't get up, Apostolis! We're not talking about you. Lida and I here are just resolving our internal issues in the interests of foreign powers and your Hellas, too. You lie there and relax, we'll sort this out ourselves…"

Lida would not believe that I had nothing to do with it and that the doctors had decided for me, she just carried on piercing me with a hawk-like stare. In the end I felt so awkward that I burst out:

"Wish me failure on the day of the operation, if you persist in thinking I'm that bad! Go on, do it, I'm not a bit sorry for myself, if I'm not worthy of the respect and sympathy of my friends in adversity!"

I never learned what Lida wished me on the day of the operation, I never asked, in fact I didn't have the chance to. But the endless suffering which was piled on me immediately after the operation could easily prompt me to think she did not believe me…

AT THE GATES OF DEATH

…Where am I? What's wrong with me? What world am I on? Why can't I breathe? Why? I'll surely die! I'll die! How long have I not been breathing? They're not taking any notice! And they won't! I'll die… I'll die… How can it be? How can I live without breathing? This is the end! (I fathomed that I was already dead and that my feeble consciousness had sparked for the last time for a few moments before fading forever and plunging into the dense darkness of icy eternity!) I lay there submissively, without breathing, in expectation of my inevitable end. It was pitiful, of course, to say farewell to life so stupidly, lying on a table in the resuscitation unit of the Institute of Cardiovascular Surgery, but I could no longer do anything or apply myself because I had something stuck in my gullet – I could not breathe in or out, and I was gradually fading. It was disturbing. I was dying in the presence of the duty doctors – there they were, the two of them, circling around the equipment, and I was seeing them through the top of my head – for sure, in dying I had turned into one huge eye which saw it all. I was dying in broad daylight, at the beginning of autumn. Through the barely opened blinds from the high windows a feeble light was breaking through into the resuscitation unit. I was dying quietly, without anyone's support, with a tube in my mouth, to the steady knock of the respirator. No-one was having anything to do with me. Slicing the air with her well-starched uniform, a thin little narrow-shouldered nurse noisily slipped past me. The duty doctors were quietly discussing something at the bedside of another operation case. I was just lying there with my newly-operated heart and quietly dying. I could not say a word. And what would be the point of words? Firstly, no-one would believe me, especially the duty doctors, accustomed to everything. And if they believed me, what then? I am not the first to be ending my earthly life here, far from the first. Secondly, my death should not deeply move anyone here, it was just a written-off patient dying… Whom could it disturb? Some sensitive young nurse just accepted for work? She'll suddenly burst into tears, all because I just a trifle resemble her elder brother or boyfriend whom she's just quarrelled with. That's all – the Institute is quits where I'm concerned! The rest is allotted to a zinc coffin…

I thought my father and brother would find it very hard to get me a zinc coffin – it's not every day they bury me, not every day they receive in Moscow my lifeless body, it would be hard for them to know what's what. And they know Moscow only very vaguely. Father thinks everything is the same as some time when he was serving in the army, when Moscow was a cold and hungry place but there was Stalinist order in the institutions.

Stalin is long gone, there only remain the countless soulless offices created by him. There remains, like an orphan, the whole system he created, which, having fallen into the hands of pitiful successors, has become lazy, still uglier and more arrogant, and has taken to coercing people for no particular purpose, also lazily, and not like under its creator – actively and for an idea, with taste! And so it's all gone awry. Without fear of the Father-Creator, his fosterlings have started twiddling their thumbs and instead of operating to the strict classical scheme of suspicion, shadowing, Troika, execution – they have got into a rut of endless eavesdropping, warning, verbose threats, etc. etc.

Having grown decrepit, the system naturally vents its spite upon people, upon those who reared it, whom it inveigled and despoiled, whom it destroyed, and upon their descendants. But people are banging day and night, like a fish against the ice, and cannot find a way out of the situation, and those who bang their heads against the wall too wholeheartedly, the so-called ideological truth-seekers, are either isolated from the best part of society, locked in the *psikhushka*, or spewed out far across the ocean so still more malice and spleen can be sworn in their wake. That works out alright for the system, it's fine.

And commanding this masquerade is Moscow, that Moscow where father was at one time lance-corporal, where once on a bus he had his officer-class watch stolen, the watch he so treasured because an officer-class watch couldn't be obtained just like that for a lance-corporal. The thief was caught on the spot, because there were lance-corporals all around, half a bus load of them, and the clean-shaven sneak thief in a modish tie jumped off the bus at the very next stop, having got a kick in the bottom from a lance-corporal's boot polished to officer-class shine. Father knew this Moscow and actually loved it, and I knew it only from his stories. I also knew that in that Moscow there were many lonely women, young and beautiful, whom it would be very easy to fall in love with. Later, father was to be amazed for a long time at the way he had managed to tear himself away from Moscow to his village out in the sticks in the Karakums. We grew up on his stories in the post-war years. But that was long ago, and Moscow is not what it was, having spread out in all directions, encroaching on the age-old forests, once so dense and impenetrable, from which the city had once emerged and in the reign of Ivan Kalita had been rolled into a tough little nut under the bow legs of the Tatar-Mongols, who had crept up on it, only eventually to get it in the neck.

But where now are my brother and father to look in this completely different Moscow for a zinc coffin for my lifeless body? They'll be at a loss! Where are they to find it, to deliver this body for washing and mourning in the homeland, in faraway Turkmenia, where professionals will continue what will have been so amateurishly begun by the young little narrow-shouldered nurse?

To think of this was very mournful, but I confess I was dying unwillingly, and if I did not cry out, it was only because my mouth was plugged with the hateful tube of the respirator, and I had no possibility of expressing my opposition to such a state of affairs.

The time dragged endlessly, there was a steady knock from the respirator, breathing for me and for those lying together with me in the resuscitation unit. Someone was groaning softly, the doctors were softly talking among themselves, while the nurse swiftly glided about the spacious room, shivering the air in her blue uniform, starched like plaster. I had already begun to be somehow accustomed to death, to the fact that it was approaching, coming nearer to me, hovering, gently embracing my body. And if I did not quite feel myself, that was only because I had begun to feel indifferent as to whether I died or stayed; I could no longer tell the difference between these two conditions, both here and there seemed to be all one and the same! I was more and more resembling a detached observer. It was as if everything was not happening to me but to some other, completely different person.

It was as if my body had already separated from my spirit, and vice-versa, my spirit had floated from my body and was wandering beneath the ceiling, looking from above at everyone, including at my immobilized flesh, criss-crossed with sharp, shiny surgical instrumentation, and violated by death. My spirit wept softly. It was mourning for my body and so it was I myself being first to mourn my departing self… I understood that my progress into non-existence was continuing, that I myself was going to meet death, slipping without a murmur into its embrace. I was waiting for my feeble consciousness to spark finally for the last time and fade in the darkness. The respirator would not breathe for me forever, and I myself had not been breathing for all eternity, and it was only by the clock of the transient world that this eternity would last only a few seconds, several critical moments.

So it might not be boring waiting for death, to while away the time of its implacable approach, I thought up a distraction: I began to recollect what had happened to me since my arrival at the Institute of Cardiovascular Surgery, the one on Leninski Prospekt… I began, of course, with the pleasantest, with Olga (my) Nikanorovna. We kissed in the changing room and in dark corners of the Institute's corridors, we kissed insatiably, even furiously, and if one of us tried to digress, this was only a challenge to the other. Naturally, it was more often Olga (my) Nikanorovna who threw down the challenge, and I would immediately advance. Possibly, I thought all this up: both that she was challenging me, and that she was carried away by me, or rather by her love for me, and would therefore excite my fantasy-rich imagination. I could no longer help myself, and on seeing this perfectly proportioned woman, I would go submissively after her and nowhere else. That is how it was at the beginning of autumn, within the walls of a supremely boring institution, where life and death saunter freely arm-in-arm along the corridors, seeking out their own… Young Olga became a saving refuge, where I would hide from the dreary preparations for the end, from thoughts of it… The daily tests, the disturbing whispers that some would never return from resuscitation, now signified for me nothing more than the usual noise in the workshop of the printing combine where students of the faculty of journalism had to work to earn some money in the summer holidays and for industrial work experience.

When I was transferred from the stuffy four-bed ward with the symbolic number and the *fortochka* ventilation window which was warped and periodically refused to open, to the Greek in the two-bed one, this was a great blessing. True, the new ward was little more than a closet, but it had cleanliness and order. The curly-headed, dark-eyed Greek lad Apostolis and I spoke the language of mutual understanding and mutual respect, and I was the only living creature he could talk to apart from his father, of course, who came to see him every day with a parcel. Then another person appeared – Olga, Olga (his) Boguslavskaya, but he would kiss her rather than talk to her. He confessed this to me, and the short, sweet name of Olya melted on his lips like a lump of quick-dissolving sugar. I understood perfectly Apostolis' Anglo-Greek linguistic cocktail! An excellent beverage, combating the unbearable smell of walls and floors, impregnated with the suffocating duos of disinfectant and medicines. I was grateful for my saviour and treated him with due respect, although he was still a teenager. Were it not for him, I no doubt would not have lasted till the operation, but would have suffocated in ward No 6. And furthermore I am to this day thankful to God for rewarding me with that autumn of such a rare generosity of beauty, when the autumnal warmth held out for a surprisingly long time. For me, a Southerner, that weather was something like a reward for that desperate decision I had decided to make, taking the risk of placing my heart in the hands of the surgeons.

Muslims believe that after death in that world every person's good and bad deeds are weighed to determine whether he is to be blissful in the garden of Paradise or burn in the flames of Hell. And I dared to entrust these supersensitive scales to the doctors and surgeons who were to patch my interventricular septum with tiny needles and the finest threads like those used by gold thread workers, and place on my heart a synthetic patch made of that once highly fashionable nylon. So may the doctors' hands be guided by the Most High and may He not allow crooked patches!

* * *

It was my third day in the new ward, I had begun to get accustomed to it, and to my neighbour also. Apostolis and I had already had time to discuss a multitude of subjects. We had, of course, talked about love, how it was with them in Greece and with us in Turkmenia. As to me, it became clear that in Greece they do not have *kalym* as we do, and they do not know about this custom. The sons of Hellas cannot see how, after marriage, you can spend years paying for your own wife!

Apostolis was in shock. In perplexity, he asked:

"What, you buy yourselves wives?"

"We don't buy them, we redeem them from their parents. Or to be more precise, we settle for the 'wisdom' of ancestors, for an ancient custom." But to myself I thought: There's something wrong here! To avoid plunging deeper into impenetrable debris, I asked him a deflecting question: "But you're a foreigner, how did you get here anyway?"

"Through the Friendship Society and our embassy," he replied, with a barely audible sigh.

"Friendship, of course, above all," I said. "But tell me, Apostolis, in your country, in Hellas, three thousand years ago, there was already Asclepius, and in Athens gold coins were being minted, at a time when in these forests here they still went about in bearskins, there were no cutting and sewing classes, so each person had to find a bear his size. And now you, proud son of Hellas, offspring of the loveliest gods, have come to us for an operation, to save yourself?"

"In our country not everyone can afford such an operation, it's very, very expensive."

"In our country it's not cheap either. Sometimes you pay with your life," I said, without going into particular details.

The dinner signal distracted us from mournful thoughts. Apostolis was fed much better than the others, and moreover for dinner he received some of the best that could be obtained from the hospital kitchen, doubtless at the expense of the Friendship Society or the embassy. We zealously followed what he was being served, the unusual variety of hospital dishes. And they were especially vigilant here about the cleanness of his bed – this was 'superintended' personally by Babka Nastya… The orderlies earnestly scrubbed the floor and would not let anywhere near our ward the 'mummy cleaners' who were taken on while their children were in the hospital awaiting an operation. These hostages' territory remained kitchen, washing-up, endless institutional corridors and other wards, while our cleaning was done by professionals, and with such zeal that their efforts soon saw the floors beginning to show signs of wear.

Thanks to Apostolis, I also managed to get to know the blessings of the Soviet medical service, highest class, so absorbingly described in school textbooks – being clothed more cleanly than others, sleeping in snow-white and not grey sheets. These acute changes gave me a certain embarrassment: whom should I thank for all this? The foreigner, really? What, is it his hospital? No, it's not his, it's ours, it belongs to me and the guys suffocating in ward No 6. But I owe my comfort to Apostolis! How can I help being embarrassed?

"I love your singer," I said, for some reason.

"Who is he?" Apostolis asked. "Meridas?"

"No, that's not him."

"Samandus?"

"No, not him either."

"Don't you remember at all?"

"I'm sorry… Just a moment. Demis! Demis Roussos!"

Apostolis' face changed.

"What's the matter, my friend?" I said with a fright.

"He is a fascist."

"He can't be! What are you saying? But what a voice! With such talent, why should he poke his nose into politics? And into a party like that…"

"It's his conviction."

"It's madness. Who would have thought?"

Here Olya (his) Boguslavskaya arrived, it was the second day of their acquaintance, and I remembered I had urgent matters that simply could not be put off. The girl blushed slightly, but did not object to my departure. When I came back after a while, Apostolis poked a finger in his chest and admitted:

"I am Comsomol!"

"How's that?" Olya (his) Boguslavskaya and I exclaimed with one voice.

"Not here, but in Greece!" Apostolis explained solemnly.

Olya (his) Boguslovskaya and I were, of course, pleased to have our own Comsomol member from Hellas, and we looked upon Apostolis as a young Olympian god.

Next day our Comsomol member was visited by his father together with some unknown man in a white coat thrown over his shoulders. They came into the ward, sat on our beds, and the young man (a Greek, from the look of him) started talking to me in excellent Russian and asked me about hospital conditions.

I willingly replied, but out of the corner of my eye I noticed that the livelier our conversation became, the more concern Apostolis displayed. He became excited, looking now at me, now at the window, sighing deeply and clutching his operated chest.

Finally, seizing the moment, he beckoned me into the corridor.

"What's happened?" I asked in surprise, looking at his blanched face.

"For God's sake, don't say anything in his presence. Or about what I told you yesterday."

"What are you talking about?"

"That I'm a Comsomol."

"Will Father be angry?"

"No, not Father," said Apostolis, and, indicating with a look the door behind which the visitors remained, added: "That man is no good. He is from the embassy. He doesn't like the Comsomol. He doesn't like the USSR."

"But he speaks Russian fluently, if only everyone did!"

"It's his business. His living."

"Based on dislike?"

"In this there is nothing out of the ordinary… He's an exile, he left Greece during the Black Colonels' coup. He came to your country, but here he became almost a fascist himself. A metamorphosis!"

"How did it happen?"

"Father says Demokrit – that's his name – saw communism in your country and now he cannot forgive himself for loving the word for so many years and giving so much of himself to this ideal."

"From love to hate in one step."

Apostolis fell silent. When we had said goodbye to the guests, he told me Demokrit was a bachelor and spent all his money on wine and women. His father was unhappy – with all this drinking and dancing to Demis Roussos every day.

"But why doesn't his father leave him?"

"Nowhere else to go. No money for a hotel. He spends it all on me…"

* * *

Meanwhile I was dying, dying, realizing with some still waking section of my cerebral cortex all the hopelessness of my situation, I was dying, without the possibility of either crying out or stirring. But the most terrible thing was being totally unable to feel the pain in my body, not having the strength to either blink or move a finger. Somewhere in the depths of my brain there existed, as if of its own accord, a little island of my consciousness, and on this island without any connexion between them, like a lighthouse beam, there would spark episodes of my pre-operation life…

"What size shoe do you take?" Vitya asked me the first day I found myself in ward No 6, looking somehow strangely at my slippers.

"Forty-one" I replied. I could not imagine what sort of question this was, why Vitya had asked it of me, and how I was to know the significance of the shoe size in the lives of those waiting their turn for an operation.

There were four of us in the ward: Vitya – old-timer at the Institute, who was now in his third month languishing here, Akhliman – a tall, sixteen-year-old lad from the Trans-Caucasus (I will now never be able to forget his kind eyes all my life) and Slava – son of a Urals miner, pupil of a vocational technical college and hence, as he introduced himself – a sociable lad. That was what he said, smiling with his grey eyes which took on a green hue the broader the smile on his little round face with its weak chin. He was the oldest in the ward before I got there.

"You've got a hard year," said Vitya in his pleasant, teenage tenor voice, having learned my shoe size.

"What do you mean?" I asked in surprise.

"You'll have a hard time, most likely. You said yourself you take a forty-one."

"Yes, a forty-one. What of it?"

"Here's your 'what of it': the operation will be hard, like the year forty-one."

"I don't get you, Vitya," I mumbled, embarrassed, looking at his sickly pale face with sandy fluff on the chin.

He raised his head from his pillow and immediately let it down.

"It means… There is one sign here… Actually there are many different signs! It's a superstition, you see, that what your shoe size is tells you how that year's weight will fall on you at the operation."

"Strange. Don't believe it."

"You don't have to, matter of choice…"

"But do you believe it?"

"At first I didn't, I didn't want to believe it… But I've been lying here so long, I've come to believe it, I've seen too much of everything… Sometimes it's like this – you look for a reason, an explanation, and you just find it. It's hard to believe but then you think, but why – was the scalpel not turned right or something…"

"But what size do you take?"

"Thirty-nine."

"Well, what do you divine from that?"

"What divining? It's all clear and confirmed. The year thirty-nine – uncertainty: there will be war, there won't be war – nothing clear, utter fog. Just uncertainty – so here I am mooning about for the last three months. And before that I spent four months lying about, also pointlessly."

"But why? Why don't they operate?"

"Just because! They don't, that's all! They won't get down to it, just promises, promises. I'm fed up. I'm behind in my class. And I'm not up to studying, anyway."

I felt really full of pity for Vitya.

"And what have you got?" I asked a fragile, big-eyed little boy with a melodious, plaintive-singing tenor voice.

"A valve has to be changed."

Next day, as we were walking in the Institute's park, Vitya told me his story, why he had decided on the operation. He and Natasha, a class mate and near neighbour, loved each other, dreamed and wrote letters. But it turned out badly. There was a medical examination in class, and one of the doctors blurted out: "Poor thing, so young and so sick…" And that was it. Natasha burst into tears, missed school next day, and then came, but that made Vitya even worse. They broke up. No more letters or dreams. That was the rather banal story. But Vitya did not have another girl, and when he remembered her he would nearly burst into tears and resemble a pitiful incubator chick.

It was the third or fourth day of my stay at the Institute. We were in full complement – Vitali, Akhliman, Slava and I. Some were lying, others sitting on their beds. Slava seemed to be day-dreaming. On Akhliman's bedside cabinet the 'Speedola' was playing some sad song, not in Russian, and in the cabinet lay some Nakhichevan pomegranates – big, matt-red ones. The cabinet was closed but I could see in. The ruby-red pomegranates lay in a heap and were bleeding. I looked them over, stopped at one of them and mentally ordered Akhliman to pass me that pomegranate. He raised himself with one elbow on his pillow, opened the cabinet, fetched the fruit I fancied and threw it across the whole ward onto my bed. In doing so, his elbow chanced to knock the 'Speedola' but he immediately managed to catch it just by the floor. Or rather, to soften its fall, but everything luckily ended without mishap.

Buffing up the skin, I asked:

"Akhliman, what is your connexion with that Jamalov?"

He answered me in Azerbaijani:

"Ol bizim chetdendir.[1]

"Really?"

"Menim atam burda olufdur onlaryn evinde, onlar bir birini taniyir."[2] Then he switched to Russian: "He promised to take me for operation with his team. Father talked to him. He is good man," he added, thinking awhile. "We brought him good pressant."

I did not know if they gave their present to Jamalov, the doctor in charge of our ward, or only planned to do so if the operation was a success.

And now I shall never know – Akhliman never returned to the ward from resuscitation. He died there under the even knock of the apparatus for artificial respiration and blood circulation…

He was dying, most probably, just like me, without anyone's help, lying on his back, all entangled with wires and tubes, penetrating even his bladder, he was dying not in the least concerned about metabolism, with a horse's dose of narcotic in his blood, with burns and bumps on the back of his head from the electrodes to awaken the heart the moment it is restarted.

I remember Akhliman in the ward watching me share out the pomegranate. He smiled his broad, kindly smile and said:

"I don't know why – I'm very, very sad."

"What? Be a man!" I tried to reassure him. But looking into his eyes, I was horrified: in his eyes, dark as currants, the grief of death was already concentrated. I could not help being frightened. I looked

---

1 He is from our parts. (Azerb.)

2 Father stayed with them, they know one another. (Azerb.)

in horror at Akhliman, as if at Satan choosing himself a destiny. "Relax!" I pronounced coolly and added: "It'll all go OK! No need to grieve so."

But I already understood – death awaited Akhliman. He was predestined to die…

I did not like that Jamalov, his compatriot. He tried to bargain with me.

"Do you wish to be operated on by the Institute's very best surgeon?" he asked, catching me not far from the staff physician's office, on the landing. He asked me hurriedly, as if incidentally, but ingratiatingly. "If you promise not to make trouble, I can arrange it for you. I don't do it for anyone, it's not done here – everyone's equal, but I've seen your father visiting you, an old man, sorry for him – he seems a good man. He must be going through a lot – he's from the East. Perhaps he used to be a bashlyk director? Ah?" he added, as if joking. At that moment his straight-facedness did not save the situation, both his fleshy chin and his belly somehow protruded treacherously, and his dark eyes behind unusually long, thick lashes, looked past me. Jamalov only seldom looked me in the eye.

I was unpleasantly embarrassed by this conversation, I was confused, and felt like a girl being importuned right in the street.

"Don't worry," I just managed to reply. "It wouldn't be nice in front of the others, they might be offended on account of me…"

I said this sincerely, but Jamalov seemed to understand it in his own way and gave me an unkind look."

"As you know best, suit yourself," he said and walked away pompously.

I was frightened: what if this incident harms me? What if no-one undertakes to operate on me at all? Or Jamalov arranges for novices to start practising on me? Goose pimples crept over my skin and all day I did not feel myself. Now, listening to Akhliman, I convinced myself: "No, the Institute's best surgeon could not be friends with a man like Jamalov, and if he was, he'd be like him too!"

Poor Akhliman, he had either already passed the expensive present to Jamalov or was planning to do so. He was sitting in front of me, having already signed his death sentence, having believed the fairy tales and arranged things with a venal character from his parts. "Should I tell him not to try and get in the Jamalov team? Would he believe me? No, most likely he wouldn't believe me. So best not say anything, they're compatriots. Why take away the hope?"

There was nothing to be done. The day after our conversation Akhliman went off to die under the scalpel of his compatriot, a talentless butcher. Looking at me in dumb reproach were Akhliman's slippers – size that fateful number forty-one…

When the lad was taken away, slightly inebriated by the pain-killing injections, he managed to say goodbye to us with a feeble half-asleep smile. Akhliman was already on the way to the operating theatre, while his slippers were left to await their owner in the ward, under his bed. Their pointed toes were levelled at me. I thought – if they had eyes how would they look? And at that very moment eyes appeared in the footwear: red, weeping, immobile… Although they were looking without reproach, I felt weird. Rot! It's not true, I told myself, and the eyes disappeared. In their place there just remained the holes for the laces.

Akhliman was awaited not only by his slippers, moved daily by the cleaner's mop, but also by the pomegranates in the bedside cabinet, an incompletely read book and his favourite torch. But the owner of all these things had been absent for more than three days. The time dragged agonizingly, the wait was torment for all of us. It was as if time had actually stopped from the moment when, depressed by the narcotics, he was taken by the young nurses on the trolley to the operations block.

The resuscitation unit was one floor above our department, but for some reason they were in no hurry to let him back from there to us. So we waited. Vitya, Slava and I and those slippers too… Then something strange started to happen, I dreamed or fancied – it is not quite clear, but it has happened like that before, although long ago, it is true. Before my eyes his slippers grew, increased in size, swelled. The others seemed to notice it too. Towards the dusk of another day, with now growing alarm we would look at the slippers, as if expecting a miracle of them, as if those slippers could, were obliged to save Akhliman.

They had already taken his clothes from the top of the bed, and to reassure us they said: "When they bring him back to the ward we'll fetch another lot of clothes." Jamalov took the Speedola and Akhliman's father – the torch. Akhliman had kept it under his pillow and used to play with it in the evenings – he loved to shine the beam along the walls and across the ceiling. A child! He said in their country, in Nakhichevan, such torches were not to be found, but ones like that were very necessary to him, and his friends loved them. "You see," he would say, "I bought it in GUM my very first day in Moscow, I was lucky…"

But we waited and waited for his return from resuscitation. Eyeing us in the corridors, the women would worryingly whisper about something. In the evening of the third day the duty doctor did not come out of the resuscitation unit, only the nurse remained on that floor, and the doctor never once came down to us. In the morning of the fourth day in our department a kind of alarming hassle began, expressed in silent glances and whisperings of the grown-ups. But we still waited, because the slippers were still in the ward – so Akhliman had not died, his body was still fighting. If that were not the case – they would have taken away his slippers as well. In the Institute there was an unwritten rule: slippers are not to be taken away while the person is alive. Might this superstition have come from the fact that we had to go for walks in our own shoes? Just try and come in wearing your own shoes, go along the corridor and enter a ward in a different medical institution with a decent antiseptic standard – they'd hardly let you in, would they?

On the fourth day nearer to lunch time Akhliman's place was occupied by another patient, but we still waited, hope remained – the slippers with the pointed toes, fashionable at that time only in the most distant villages, were still there under the bed. Suddenly I noticed (and the others – Vitya and Slavik, only no-one even said a word), that from Akhliman's bedside cabinet the dark-brown blood of the Nakhichevan pomegranates was leaking out onto the floor. It leaked and leaked, and the newcomer tossed and turned restlessly on his bed. Something disturbed him: was it the vinous smell of the fermenting pomegranate juice, or the slippers which had swelled to improbable proportions? Or perhaps something else? That same day, returning to the ward from the dining room after dinner, we saw that Akhliman's slippers had been taken away…

A DRAUGHT OF WATER

Meanwhile, I was dying. Death was not unexpected for me, I sorrowfully remembered everything I had read and heard about it, about the ascension of the soul to Heaven in the hour of decease. Of one thing I can accurately say: the desperation, intensified hundreds, thousands of times by the thought of the inevitability of departure from the terrestrial world, ascends high above one's own 'I' of sacrifice. To live, just live, to take one more little look at this life and achieve if only a thousandth part of what was achieved before and never will be anymore… Poised between life and death, I saw my own nothingness reflected in the distended pupils of the doctor who had been sewing up my pericardium.

Later, coming to the Institute for check-ups, I would kneel before the morose Bakulev set in stone. Fresh flowers would nearly always lie at his feet, but my flowers were never there. I spent a lot of money on bouquets both before and after the operation, but I gave them not to images but to girls. I do not think that Bakulev, were he alive, would blame me for that. Wasn't that what he fought for, going through the blood of his patients to victory, to give back to me and others the fearlessness and even some of the light-heartedness of practically healthy people? And how many souls perished under the surgical scalpels in those years, almost a decade, before Bakulev and his colleagues finally succeeded in achieving steadily successful heart operations…

* * *

My fading consciousness was out of tune with me, but it was trying to stay in the real world, it was resisting and did not wish to leave it. However, it was pining in a mortal anguish of pain and doom. In the resuscitation unit there were enough groans – mine would have been drowned inaudibly in the general choir. Soloist was a thick-set, shaven-headed man trying to utter something more or less distinctly in an Asiatic accent: he would be either giving thanks or swearing, but each time he would start with the name of Allah, the only One, before Whom his non-European mind would bow.

I once believed in God, too, in my distant childhood when at every step I was relentlessly pursued by my own vain hopes. I used every day, on my own, to conquer great distances on my donkey in the desert. Only there, in a tiny oasis I had discovered among the sand dunes, was there enough grass, for which I would wander so far. All around was a world I had not yet come to know and understand completely: a world of humming and silence, wild and tender, sultry and cool, as lovely as the flowers of the camel thorn, and stinging like its thorns. Such was the stern reality. But earlier still (before that we lived in a different place) there was a little girl, Aya – of my age, of whom I had vague memories. At that time many said people would soon have to chew earth or even eat each other because certain satraps had forbidden people to keep animals for themselves – sheep and cows and camels alike, and the ban on horses was issued even earlier – under Stalin. They said Stalin was fiercer than the present one, but he was dead and the present one was so far alive, although he too would soon either be killed or sent to America. They said he was very friendly with the Americans and wanted to sell us all to them for the secret of growing maize, and furthermore that he had a direct telephone line to America on which he was blurting out our secrets. Aya and I had little idea what the grown-ups were talking about, and having heard enough, we used to go out and play and seek out a cosy little place where our elders would not poke their noses, and hide so no-one could interfere. Once we hid behind some gates leaning against the fence. It never occurred to anyone that anything living could squeeze in there, apart from kittens. Aya only had knickers on, which would fall down from time to time.

When we were behind the gates, Aya once again failed to pull up her knickers and they were just left to swing against her chubby little knees. I was at a loss, but Aya did not even think of being embarrassed. Quite the reverse, she stared at me, as if expecting some sort of action on my part. I did not know what she wanted and why she suddenly lay on the ground… But I remember with what curiosity the little girl gaped at me. I indecisively took the pliable stalk the little girl had pointed at me and twisted it, without realizing why it had been given to me. Aya prompted me: she took my hand holding the stalk, placed it on her belly and then slowly drew it below her navel. That was how we started having fun, I tickled her body with the stalk, and Aya watched me carefully. "Not so hard!" she instructed me, and I obediently followed her promptings. But there came a time when I got impatient and hurt Aya. She screamed, crept out of our hiding place and, with a wild howl, ran home. Her mother was already rushing towards her, and she caught me the very moment my head poked out of the crevice. She chucked me out of the hiding place by my ears – since then I've been going about with crumpled ears!

I saw Aya many, many years later. She was a *gaytarma* – she married and after the honeymoon she returned to the parental nest for good.

"How're things?" I asked Aya. "Everything alright?"

She blushed crimson, remembering the same things as I did, no doubt, and then burst into tears.

"I didn't want to wed, I wanted you."

* * *

I'm on my way home now, sitting above the grass on my tired white ass and still thinking of Aya and her chubby little knees. Why, if she rode with me every day such a distance, she might lose weight. As they haven't either a cow or sheep she will always be a little fatty, and I don't like them like that…

The road is difficult, the day is sultry – nearly fifty in the shade and only Allah knows what in the blazing sun! All around is desert, there is nowhere to shelter and we just keep going. The donkey can hardly move her feet, she is dying as she walks. In the distance is a row of mulberry trees, but how can we reach them? The donkey will die before she covers a third of the way. Without my white ass I too will die. I ride half asleep and half dead, tormented with thirst. I was languishing with the heat an hour ago, when I had finished cutting the grass. I don't remember how I loaded it on the ass – how did I find the strength? I ride and pray Allah not to take my donkey. I ride, my gaze fixed on the mulberry trees on the horizon. Don't collapse, just get to the mulberry trees, there can't fail to be water there! But my white ass must have water at once, this minute! How can I explain to her that there will be water but not a drop yet! Midday. Gadflies. Buzzing. Thirst dries the heart, my voice has already gone, or it never was, my tongue is swollen and cleaves to the roof of my mouth. I try chewing *suvot*, water grass, but its name is deceptive: it is bitter and unpleasant, when chewed it smells of stagnant water and when you try and spit it out – you can't.

The salutary trees are swaying on the horizon like a vision from *A thousand and one nights*, like a mirage. Am I perhaps hastening there for nothing? Anyway, I am going that way and the strides of my white ass hardly resemble haste. It is the walk of an exhausted, half-dead animal. The elders say whoever dies of thirst in the desert is a martyr. The place where he is buried is specially marked. And travellers passing by leave silver coins on the martyr's solitary grave. My dehydrated, tormented body feels that I am already not far from such happiness, it is only a pity that the silver coins will not come to me: others will leave them and others will pick them up! With my benumbed tongue I try to pronounce suras from the Koran. Believing in their sacred working power, I try to shorten the distance between the mulberry trees and us, me and my long-suffering white ass. In the shade of the mulberry trees there is water, there absolutely must be! In my heart I feel that the mulberry trees in their salutary shade preserve for the afflicted some remnant of water in an old *aryk*.

"Oh, Allah, All-Merciful!" I pray. "Make it so there is water there! I will get there, we will get there! Me and my donkey, my white ass! Make it so we get there."

We trudge on, step after step, each harder than the last, the resonant knock of hoof on *takyr*, the cracked, dried hard earth, is heard more and more infrequently.

"Oh, Allah, make it so I grow a bit quicker and become taller, then Gozel will love me and stop thinking I'm still little. Make it! Can't you? What kind of Almighty are you then? Fine, I'll grow somehow myself, but save me, give me water! If we can't get to the trees at all, make it so they move to meet us, can't you? What, is it hard for you? Look, we're dying of thirst!"

But the mulberry trees still loom in the haze – they just haven't come any nearer. The noonday sun hangs over the world like a curse, sparing no-one. Time has become tangible, like a fire-breathing dragon. A lizard, the '*gune gargan*', has climbed onto a saxaul twig and is gulping the hot air with open mouth, ejecting its narrow, rough little tongue. She is looking at us with fear and hostility, as if it is my white ass and I who have drunk all the water of the Karakums. Silly 'gune gargan' lizard, why curse us, curse the sun, that's your job according to your name!

I run the last few metres to the mulberry trees, leaving my white ass to be tormented by the gadflies which have attacked us as we approached the trees. I run headlong, I run with all my remaining strength, killing myself with these last few steps. The old mulberry trees, growing along the narrow, dried-up old *aryk*, turn out to be planted much further apart than it appeared from afar. How drearily and sadly they look at me with their droopy, dusty leaves. I jump into the bed of the *aryk* and prostrate myself on the ground. It's dry… But it feels as if water has been here, has been! Maybe last week, maybe a month ago, but it surely has been! I run along the *aryk*, heart bursting, and in my dry throat there gurgles the question: where is there somewhere a bit deeper? There must be somewhere in the *aryk* where water has been preserved! I walk in desperation, using strength I have drawn from I know not where, and finally, I fall on my knees before a tiny sheet of stagnant water. I prostrate myself at the water. A large olive-grey toad with dark-green spots directs her gaze at me imploringly, evidently concerned for her little black tadpole brood. The puddle is toad-chin-deep. But I must drink the water or I die! The toad's white pendulous crop goes up and down excitedly. Up and down, up and down! It keeps on. My eyes grow dim. I can't bear to look any longer. I grab the toad and throw her a little way from the puddle, and prostrate myself once more to what's left of the water. The mistress of the puddle bears no grudge: as if nothing has happened, she approaches me once more with little jumps, watches, waits to see – will I leave just a little water for her and her brood, just for a day's life? But I am not capable of stopping, I keep on drinking the stagnant water, the level decreases implacably, until finally it disappears altogether. The black tadpoles, waggling the tails which have not yet dropped off them, quiver helplessly in the thick marshy ooze left at the bottom of the puddle. Drugged with the water I have drunk, I get up and, swaying, look pointlessly around. Then I slowly leave the place where there was recently a decent puddle, where I reckon the green toad's brood will have another day or two to live. I go, and watching me go, goggling her eyes and gulping the sultry air, is the unlucky toad…

* * *

Over there, where the dry earth merges with the dry heavens, jackals have raised a howl. They are howling with a menacing sadness, ever more frantically, and my heart listens to those sounds with a sinking feeling, foreseeing nothing good. What is wrong with them? Why have the jackals, forgetting their age-old fear of daylight, suddenly started howling in the presence of the sun? What need has lured them out of their dark, stinking holes? My donkey, my white ass, dilates her nostrils and snorts, she rolls her big, crazed eyes as big as apples, she revolts and tries to break away and rush into panic-stricken flight. I am afraid to be left on my own with this howling, under the parched sky, to single-handedly face the infuriated jackals which are going out of their minds for some unknown reason. There's nothing good to be expected of them! The donkey is not much of a comrade, but there's no choice, we'll try and break out of this Hell together. God forbid she should leave me and run away – it would be my death.

* * *

But I was dying. Dying in my prime, fully conscious, lying in the resuscitation department of cardiovascular surgery. Young little nurses scurried around, stirring the autumn air with their stiffly starched blue uniforms. The duty doctors talked quietly. They were tired, exhausted, with the usual dark rings under their eyes, with phonendoscopes ready hanging on their chests, and their fingers smelling of tobacco.

I was dying, dying silently, without a single groan, cry or complaint, because breathing, making a noise and complaining for me were the breathing and blood circulation machines, and a countless miscellany of wires and tubes linking my body with them were my last hope of life. Worn out by my own inactivity, I began to sink ever deeper into a cold sweaty gloom. Everything I could and did see before had disappeared, and there remained only what I remembered, what I could take with me into any distance, any dimension, into any space – that which really constituted me myself, my past inseparable from me: my green toad, my jackals, the '*gune gargan*' lizard and my white ass…

Exhausted from asphyxia, from lack of oxygen, writhing impotently on my hard and narrow berth, I only tried to turn onto my side – and immediately collapsed into an abyss right under the hooves of my white ass. My heart started thumping madly, my eyes rolled into my forehead, my eyelashes were already swimming in a cold sweat. I shrank, finding myself barely two fingers from my sure destruction, from death. And she was coming ever closer to me, tormenting, taunting me and settling past scores.

The stony hoof of the abominably stubborn animal (not for nothing do they say "stubborn as an ass") hung over me. It was a hind hoof, and now, raised above the ground, it was bound to descend upon my belly, and accomplish its bloody deed. My breathing stopped, my eyes were wide open and arms and legs spread faint-heartedly on the ground. What must be accomplished must be accomplished, for it was now impossible to change anything. I knew that by stepping with its hoof on my belly, just above the navel, my white ass (in whom I at last recognized my angel of death, my Azrael) would without any compunction complete what she had begun, after which I would be left to die an agonizing death at midday on the dusty path… And my white ass will have done her black deed, that is her nature, after all, and she could hardly be accused of murder. Having dropped the heavy half-moon of her hoof on my belly, and pressing it down with all her weight, she will inevitably have to raise her other leg, thus intensifying the murderous pressure. In the twinkling of an eye the tissue of my body will have been ripped apart when the hoof penetrates inside, churning up the innards and breaking vitally important links. I would anyway be left a lifeless worm when she moved her foot.

In dumb horror I watched as one of those hooves descended upon me, hooves which had once measured out hundreds or maybe thousands of kilometres of sultry steppe, carrying me for grass and back. And now it was my death. Everything was now irreversible. For a moment I believed that death was a completely natural retribution for my having for so many years ridden on the back of my angel of death, for the self-abasement which Azrael must have felt, carrying me on her, assuming the aspect of my white ass. But won't my good deeds be taken into account, when I would often save the ass from pain and lameness, winkling out of her hooves bits of glass or sharp stones which had got stuck in?

But the hoof kept coming down and down, it had now come close to the decisive margin, it had crossed it, and had slowly crept a millimetre at a time, a hundredth of a millimetre at a time, agonizingly prolonging the last second of my life. The very last one! That moment dragged on so cruelly long that to this day I seem to have been eternally under the hoof of my ungrateful white ass, whom I had fed the sweetest grass my land could ever grow.

Ravaged by the prolonged wait for inevitable death, I was now almost ready to accept it. But suddenly something happened within me – within my soul, my heart, my memory: I pulled myself together, strained with all my body and turned into a knot of life! With improbable strength, in the twinkling of an eye, I bent my knees, and all my exhausted muscles started to work in tandem and I swiftly rolled out from under the hooves one millionth of a second before destruction.

* * *

The lamp hanging above me flashed on. I wanted to turn and protect myself from the light blazing in my eyes, but someone stopped me. The feel of extraneous material on my body (rubber gloves) reminded me where I was and made me keep still in expectation. Nurse Larisa began to adjust the catheter, ensuring a steady flow of urine into the urine bag hanging to the right of the table on which my reviving body lay. She was occupied for a long time, she could not get something right, and so her every movement gave me intolerable pain. I tried to defend myself, bending my legs. Then, leaving for a while her fruitless efforts, the nurse looked me in the eye in a special way, in her own way somehow, taking off her rubber gloves and doing the job in a different way. I seemed for the first time in my life to feel the warmth of feminine hands… Larisa confidently pushed the catheter into the long-suffering member of my body. Now losing consciousness, now falling into normal sleep, I saw the bloody fluid flowing and filling the bag and Larisa leaving my table, then coming back in mid-turn and putting her tongue out at me. I tried in response to form a smile, but darkness once again extinguished my consciousness which had been about to blaze up for a moment in a flame as red as Larisa's tongue.

I awoke once more in the dark, in silence. Only sometimes someone would intermittently give a muffled groan on a far table. Arrayed in a row at my bed head, the devices of continual control of blood pressure and pulse were monitoring me. In their vague spectral luminescence I suddenly saw my distant past: a hot Turkmen midday and myself, aged seven or eight…

Mummy and I were drinking tea, sitting in the shade of the overhanging vine. Nearby the hearth was smouldering, lazily wafting towards us from time to time the bitter-sweet smoke of camel dung. In the grey ash our favourite *kumgan* glowed, and although smoked with age, the water boiled in it made tea so flavoursome there was none more flavoursome in the whole wide world. The weather was so hot that the just-brewed tea did not seem so very hot. I drank it from a red *pialushka* bowl decorated with cockerels, taking big draughts and watching the tea leaves floating upright – that means visitors.

Then from behind a pile of saxaul firewood, at our gates there appeared two people – an old woman and a girl of about my age. They continued on their way, as if not noticing us and had already reached the middle of the gates. The little girl suddenly looked at us and said something to her companion. They stopped, and two pairs of eyes stared in our direction, as if in expectation of being invited in. And an invitation followed, so the travellers did not have to languish for long at the gates in uncertainty.

"Salamalik," said Mummy, greeting the venerable old woman, and with a hospitable gesture she indicated the *koshma* rug.

"Amanmy, how are you, daughter?" responded the latter, taking her seat.

"Don't be shy, come into the shade," Mummy encouraged the tired travellers. "You come, too, little girl." Mummy almost forced the little black-haired girl with two little pigtails sticking out to sit next to me. "Make yourselves comfortable."

"Peace be upon your house!" said the old woman, starting to politely ask questions of Mummy. "How is your health, daughter? How are your children? Is the Master at home?"

"Glory to Allah, all is well!" Mummy replied.

"Are your relatives and neighbours alive and well? How are your animals? May all sickness pass you by!"

"All is well with us, everything is in order," Mummy observed the ritual, nodding affirmatively in time with the conversation.

Then came her turn to ask questions, and Mummy asked the old woman in detail about everything, receiving patient answers in exchange.

As soon as the girl had drunk her tea with a sweet *lepioshka,* the grown-ups sent us into the house, telling us to have a nap in the cool, darkened room, from which Mummy had chased the noisome flies early that morning. And the grown-ups remained in the arbour, to linger over their tea a little longer and wait for the heat to abate, as the old woman and the little girl still had no short distance to travel. They were making for one of the distant villages, so they were glad to accept the invitation to rest in the shade. Travelling without caution in such baking heat was simply unthinkable – the old woman was worried her niece might get a headache from the searing heat or a nosebleed from sunstroke.

I was struck by the unusual green, slanting eyes of this swarthy little girl, I did not know how to escape her intense gaze. The visitor had been staring at me even in the arbour, but when we were left on our own in the half-darkened room, she simply never took her eyes off me. Their shine seemed mysterious and strange to me. I was overcome by hitherto unknown, disturbing feelings. I trembled, I was actually afraid. Alongside me lay a little girl, but I had the persistent feeling that l had been locked in all alone with a black cat. The girl transfixed me with the intense gaze of her big green eyes, throwing me more and more into confusion. But it turned out that her glances were not everything. They were only little flowers, the main thing awaiting me was yet to come. I recoiled when she tenaciously took me by the hand. My heart started beating madly, I dared neither object nor take my hand away. But I gradually began to thaw: I felt the tenderness of touch, I sensed that the girl was weaker, and I became bolder. A new feeling wafted over me, whose mysterious magnetic force I had cautiously avoided hitherto… My heart, which had barely calmed down, started beating hard again. And then this is what happened: I took her hands in mine and snuggled up to the little girl. She looked at me still just as fixedly and kept silence, displaying a strange submissiveness. I was well aware that not only did boys avoid girls, the latter did not allow boys to approach them, and they would not allow anyone to take them by the hands. So I found the behaviour of the little guest in permitting unheard-of bodily proximity all the more of a mystery. Unfamiliar feelings awoke in me – I moved closer and closer to the little girl… She began stroking my coarse, curly hair. I could now hardly understand it – she was breathing right next to me, and her eyes looked at me with a challenge, almost mockingly. Remembering everything I knew at that time from conversations of grown-ups and stories told by my peers and street pals, I drew my lips close to her fine little lips like pistachios. Every second I earnestly expected her to push me away. But rebuff did not follow, and our lips came together, as a bee and a nectar-bearing flower come together early in the morning. Only once did the little girl cry out…

Just a little later I saw the result of our bold proximity, when we were woken, as it were, without having slept – Keklik's lips were aglow like a suddenly opened little crimson bud. Strange were my feelings from the sudden change which had occurred in the darkened room with my little guest in a space of time we were unaware of. Ah, how sweet it was – our childish 'dream'.

Understandably, it was for me to see the guests to the country road, so I still had a long way to walk alongside Keklik. All the way, she looked at me stealthily, without taking her eyes off me. But all the time I looked away in confusion, fearing her grandmother might guess our terrible secret and punish us both. Only now and again, plucking up my boyish courage, did I manage to raise my eyes and respond to the little girl's glance. My hands, cheeks and lips were aglow with shame – I was agitated. Although Keklik wore that same little old dress faded from the sunlight and her two pigtails stuck up so perkily, her eyes… her unusual green eyes were shining already like a grown-up's!

All my life I have remembered that little girl, who instilled an unearthly longing in my eyes. Perhaps that is why all the women I met later on fell into despair because it was not they but someone else who was destined to leave a trace in my spirit. But even curbing somewhat their time-worn feminine jealousy, they would endeavour to console me, as if trying to oust the image of that distant… But I would still seek in women perchance a hint of the lineaments of her who, in my distant childhood, looked deep into my soul, horrifying me and then crying

out quite unchildishly, lost in a game which she herself had started...
My little visitor, where are you?

* * *

Once destiny relented.

I was on my way back to Moscow after the winter holidays. Emotions still seethed in my soul, and I had not managed to cubby-hole my impressions of my short meeting with the Motherland. Passing along the interior of the supersonic airliner to take my seat, I suddenly halted, sensing a penetrating gaze at myself. It was She. Hardly had our eyes met than we immediately recognized each other: there could be no mistake. Even in total darkness we would have found each other – for all these years we had been bound to each other invisibly by an eerie childhood secret!

We sat side-by-side and talked. Keklik stunned me immediately in every way: her provocatively striking appearance and her eloquence. It turned out that Keklik was flying to defend a thesis on her subject – she worked as a venereologist. And very shortly, with her stark medical terminology (with a superfluity of cynicism) she was to leave me completely at a loss, revealing my total ignorance of the subject of the conversation. My travelling companion, in contrast to her prototype of long ago – the silent little girl – now spoke at length and pleasurably and to beautiful effect: her lips enticed, her bosom rose, beneath her elegantly cut dress lived a resilient body... But an unspeakable Grief fell on me. It was evident that Keklik was no longer the same one, a self-confidence had long ago taken root in her, but I somehow contrived to detect a trait relating her to that little visitor – a willingness to yield. I instantly caught it in her green cat-like eyes, and having focused on them, no longer removed my gaze from them.

The noise of the aircraft engines on landing had not yet fallen completely silent in our ears, when Keklik sweetly, graciously stretched herself on the divan in my bachelor-style quiet, cosy post-graduate room. The act of love did not last long, her refined mastery in bed eclipsed the very memory of the childhood love I had carefully treasured from that first meeting. So I very soon became convinced that I could never find in this Keklik even a hundredth part of what she once was in my innocent embraces. I realised I was doomed all my life to search for the one who had visited my soul at a time of sensual awakening, knowing beforehand that I would now never succeed in finding her.

* * *

Leaving behind her not only the trace of her lovely body on the official postgraduate divan, but also profound confusion in my soul, Keklik once again evaporated like medical ether…

My nose was assaulted by the mixed smell of medicines unknown to me! The salutary ray of a bright memory once again clove the darkness of approaching death, snatching me from its bony paws. Having barely escaped the very worst that could await me, I was actually poised above the abyss between present and past, as I was once, in my distant childhood, trying to prove my bravery by walking along a narrow log over Firyuzinka torrent.

My dispersing consciousness suddenly grasped at another name dear to my heart – Anetta, the little girl from the pioneer camp in the Firyuza mountain valley. My recollections of Anetta and her image used sometimes to become confused with the figure of that unique one from my distant childhood, but now her image seemed to have rebelled in protest without submitting to the laws of time. Little pictures of her would float ever more insistently above the horizon of my dim memory in the first fresh richness of my palette of feelings as it was many years ago.

And, still lying in the resuscitation ward, not only as if awake did I suddenly hear the babbling of the river, I was actually swept by that summer mountain coolness, and I found myself in the place where I first met my princess, whose name, the further away, the more it rose up from the fluster of past days.

* * *

She appeared unexpectedly and unforeseen.

In the period after lunch, when total silence reigned in the pioneer camp – the dead hour – I was sitting by the gates under the arbour sunshade, as befits someone on duty. At this hour everyone is asleep and there is only the gurgling of the Firyuzinka, the ice-cold mountain stream which, descending from the peaks of the Kopet-Dag, merrily runs past our camp down through the village, bringing bracing coolness to everyone coming to this mountain valley. Age-old plane trees rose up in a row along the Firyuzinka, rustling their leaves in thanks for the life bestowed by the stream.

And suddenly the little fretted wicket-gate opened and She entered…

"I'm Anetta," the thin little girl introduced herself, emerging from behind the back of a tall woman in an old-fashioned straw hat.

"I'm Nazarli…" I pronounced shyly, taking her delicate little hand.

"Go on, Anettka, get settled in, you're in block five, and I'll go and talk to the director." Then the old-fashioned hat addressed me, too: "Boy! Help her take the suitcase, she's such a skinny little thing of ours, God forbid she should strain herself any more. But here in the camp I think she'll get better."

"Now, Auntie!" the little girl drawled in embarrassment.

Not taking any notice of what her niece had said, the woman continued:

"It's so cool in your parts, just wonderful! Not for nothing is it called Firyuza, meaning turquoise, eh?" In Ashkhabad the asphalt is already melting in the morning, we help ourselves with musk melons and water melons from the fridge. Go on, why am I telling you all this rubbish when you've all come from there?"

"No, we're not all from the capital," I retorted. "There are some from other places too. I've come from a distant *kolkhoz*, it's even hotter there. At midday roast camels walk the streets there! And further on there are the Karakums…"

The old-fashioned hat laughed shrilly, she liked my joke so.

"I never knew camels, especially roast ones, roamed the streets anywhere. You must have come from really far away, boy. It's a good thing at least someone lives there, or it'd be just sand and saxaul all over…"

I was going to try and tell her something else, but did not manage to.

"So take the suitcase and go, what are we standing here 'blah-blahing' for? Take Anetta to the place! And I'll be on duty instead of you. I'll have a rest, go on," she waved her hand, adding: "And you boy, keep calm, and don't forget to ask the senior person in charge to come here."

So I carried her little suitcase to block five itself. I do not remember ever in my life carrying such a precious load! I could not help feeling in my arms the noble weight of the cardboard suitcase entrusted to me like the diamond casket of an unearthly princess. Even the leaves of the walnut trees seemed to be playing a mysterious melody of love after just two glances from the big, enchanting eyes of Anetta, and I understood – something had happened within me, something magical. In the short time we had walked side-by-side I realized Anetta was special. Her walk was so light she seemed not to walk but float above the ground, like a feather fallen from the wing of a passing bird. She not only smiled beautifully, she even seemed to breathe in a special way. And she could laugh so shrilly for any or no reason, as I realized a little later when my sufferings for her began…

Almost throughout the season I gave her all kinds of tokens of attention, bringing her flowers, and one could say I even ran after her. But she kept me at a respectful distance, as she did all the others. A touch-me-not. Maybe she had completely forgotten I was the first to meet her here! Even on the dance floor of an evening she would amuse herself only with her girl friends, and would refuse to go for a dance with the boys. Many tried their luck, and of course l was leader in this respect, but only once in the whole long camp season did success smile upon me. That miracle occurred on the day of the closure of the camp season. Completely unexpectedly, at the very last hour when there was no hope left.

Everyone was happy. We're going home! To our parents, to normal home life, without compulsory morning exercises! Of course, home was not Firyuza with its cool, blue peaks and tinkling ice-cold rills, but still it was one's own home, one's own courtyard…

Sitting on the steps in front of my block, I was saying goodbye with a sad face to those who were happily leaving the grounds of the pioneer camp. The farewell pioneer camp fire was still smouldering, the sad celebratory pre-evening rumble was still audible. And suddenly an excited little girl's voice said:

"Boy! boy! Anetta's calling you!"

A slight shiver ran through my whole body. I looked round. Not a soul to be seen…

"Who? Me?" I asked the dusk.

At that moment I was too excited to instantaneously understand the mysterious invitation. After all, the last camp season had just finished, at the solemn parade the blood-red flag had just been lowered till next summer. And naturally all of us, me included, were under the spell of that exciting event. But my confusion instantly irritated the little bearer of the secret.

"Yes, you, you, lop ears!" From behind the walnut tree poked the head of a little girl from detachment five.

"Where does she want me? Where is she?"

"There… Follow me quick, stupid!" The little girl skipped ahead and I ran after her. She was so fast I could hardly keep up. It was already twilight, evening was approaching. Some children were being collected by their parents who had come for the solemn closure of the camp. The parents were also overcome, some had tears in their eyes, while others smiled. The camp was by now almost deserted, only here and there lost or unclaimed children loitered on their own. We are from a faraway village, nearly half a thousand kilometres from here, we live where cotton grows, much cotton, nothing but cotton. But we still want to go home, and we wait and wait for deaf Mamedaman, our minder. On the train he may buy us cocoa and *korzhiki* biscuits and on the platform of the Ashkhabad station, waiting for our connexion, even ice-cream. Although we were already given some today for supper, in honour of the end of the season, but mind you that is something special – however much you have you can never have enough. And ice-cream here, in Firyuza and Ashkhabad, is much more delicious than ours, which is plain ice.

True, another portion of ice-cream was attractive, but I was highly disgruntled by my imminent parting with Anetta, the chosen one of my heart. I had suffered and sighed for her for so long in the hope of her favour, but she would only laugh at me. She was proud to be loved, but she didn't care a fig. She kept her girl friends amused! But what had happened now? Really? It's not possible! My heart fluttered like a little bird, I ran after the little girl who used also to laugh at me and at my clumsy advances towards her girl friend, at my sighs with which I escorted Anetta everywhere.

I ran, exulting: "My sacrifices, my endless sufferings have not been in vain! How many jibes have I been the butt of! From the children of our detachment and other detachments. They could not understand what I saw in that skinny, capricious little girl with the frighteningly pale face. I forgave them generously, because none of them could look as deeply as I could into her unfathomably blue eyes in which even an adult could well drown. Only I could see them, it was I who fell into the dangerous and beautiful field of their attraction.

Now I was flying headlong after the girl friend of my princess through the fast gathering evening gloom, which was creeping down from the mountain peaks. The little girl suddenly caught the toe of her sandal in the root of a walnut tree and tumbled in a heap on the ground, emitting a croaking sound. But without stopping for one minute, she jumped up and rushed on, shouting as she ran:

"Let's race!"

I sped up, my soul rejoicing: "Wow! What pain she's suffered so Anetta and I can get together quickly! Could I have dreamt of such a thing only yesterday? Poor thing, she fell, she could have broken her knee, but she's running and not even crying."

We crossed the whole territory of the camp. It was now completely dark. Liza – that was the name of Anetta's girl friend – ran to the ladies' toilet which was hidden beneath an old walnut tree. I stopped sharply – ahead was the ladies' toilet, where we boys were forbidden to go. Seeing I had indecisively halted on the spot, Liza waved.

"Come quick!" she cried.

I ran up to her.

"Where, into the ladies?"

"Blockhead," Liza strained through her teeth. Where else? Of course, into the ladies! Did you think she was going to run after you into the men's? What were you thinking of?"

I cautiously approached the doors.

"Yes, go on, don't be afraid! I'll keep guard for you."

I went in. Inside it was still darker. Pressing myself against the wall, I took several uneasy steps forward… Unexpectedly, someone took me by the hand and drew me along.

"This way…"

"Anetta!"

"Yes, yes… This way!"

"Anetta!"

I saw her in the corner, where a narrow strip of light fell on her from above, through a crevice in the roof. Anetta was terribly excited, her big eyes gave out a blue-grey radiance. I froze indecisively. At that moment I was frightened: the little girl's eyes burned so bright in the August evening darkness – was it really I who had lit them?

I stepped back, but she squeezed my hand tighter.

"Boy!"

"Anetta!"

"Boy, I want, I want…" she burst into tears. "I want to give you my address. Will you remember it?"

"I will remember it!" I whispered.

"But first you may kiss me…"

And we started inexpertly kissing in that changing room, whose wooden floor was generously sprinkled with chlorine glistening in the semi-darkness. The acrid smell hit you in the eyes and nostrils, intensely irritating the airways, so our innocent kiss was very soon mixed with genuine childish tears.

"Anetta!" I exclaimed with constraint, hardly having torn myself away from her sweet lips, breathless either from the acuteness of sensual rapture, or from the sharp smell of the chlorine.

My head spun helplessly, I felt sick, I clung to the only one who could save me from an ignominious fall. It was all like a dream, yet I was awake: my hands have forever cherished the memory of that skinny little girl, her fragile little body which trembled in my artless embraces for perhaps several seconds… Several moments…

We recoiled simultaneously when Liza banged on the tinplate partition to warn of someone's approach. We fluttered like frightened little birds out of the lavatory and flew in different directions, managing as we fled to exchange two or three words, which I have since then kept treasured in my memory.

"Will you be coming next year?" I asked.

She half turned as she ran and waved.

"I'll try!" she replied, and vanished into the August night. I never met Anetta again either as a teenager or a grown-up. I lost before I could win.

Since then I have always been especially sad of an August night. I realize our life consists of losses only. Indeed, life itself – the only fragile thing of value awarded to us at birth – is it not striving to leave us, ready to fly to the heavens at any moment?

* * *

Meanwhile, death was coming ever closer. And the curious thing was, the closer it came, the sharper and brighter my memories became. My past grasped at my present, it just did not wish to part with me. Time and again, in the nooks and crannies of my consciousness, hearth cinders would flare up in which memories were stored as in vessels of precious things. And they would come to life in my memory at the critical moment when my soul was almost ready to part with my transient body. It was those long-forgotten or half-forgotten people and events that would come back to me every time before final departure.

It is strange – my flesh still rests here, in the Institute's ward, but my thoughts continue to exist separately, as if of their own accord, outside my exhausted, tormented body… The only thread linking me with life is my memories. And they are not letting me go finally to that world which, it would seem, I could easily put out my hand and touch.

POSTMAN

Late May. The twittering of steppeland birds. Buzzing. The dive-bombing flights of impetuous multicoloured wasps: yellow and brown, red and black, bane of chance passers-by. Gadflies, as usual, circle above the steppelands in search of potential victims, but success smiles on them less and less often: everything living is hiding in its lair. The tulips' tender petals have long ago been seared away, their once elegant little stalks are drooping, and only occasionally in the dawn there flash here and there the little glints of rare belated red poppies, but they too will be immediately scorched by the merciless rays of the sun, which is growing fiercer by the day.

Outlandish heat. I am 14 years old. I am the village postman. My bicycle travels the long, winding, deserted streets of the half-empty village, whose inhabitants have moved to the fields for the field season, to be nearer work. The wheels of my speedy bicycle know every pothole, every bump of these streets, which of them terminate in the steppelands and which come up against the foothills.

I prefer riding towards the mountains, I am lured by the huge shapes fading to a bluish hue in the distance, especially beautiful in the mist. But it is not bad in the direction of the steppelands, because it's downhill, there's no need to pedal, you just sit and steer. It's a pity that huge black ants scurry tirelessly about the village. I try to cycle round them, but our paths continually cross – I'm troubled when the ants are killed underneath my wheels. There always were quite a few, but now the village is deserted you cannot avoid them when walking, and even less when riding, and they have become bigger and more aggressive… But I cannot even imagine our village without giant ants.

Boredom!.. Especially now people have deserted residential areas in whole families, have forsaken everything and, like convicts, gone to the cotton for more than half a year to live like gypsies in a camp by the great water, the Karakum Canal. And what for? To earn a bit more, to buy new things, and leave them in an empty house next year!

Tedium!

It could not be said that there was no-one left in the village. There were some left: old men, old women, pregnant women and those whose presence here was simply essential while there were still living people here: there was shopkeeper Kerim, 'director' of the kerosene shop Khabip, the jealous Gulberdy with his young wife, and I. You hardly need reminding about Medic Berdy – he was obviously the most important person! He was obliged to give medical aid both to those in the field camp and to those remaining in the village, but there was no help from him for either. His exuberant inactivity could only be envied, because he was 'afire' at work. He was lucky, for there were only two premises in the village with air conditioning – one was the chairman's office, and the other was the surgery of 'slogger' Berdy. That is why he preferred to spend most of the day at the surgery, and not at home.

I have to deliver an official letter addressed to old Gulberdy, husband of a young wife. No wonder he looks at all men in the village from under his thick eyebrows with suspicion and vexation, as befits the husband of a child bride. What the message is I do not know: either Gulberdy's pension is being increased again or – for the umpteenth time – it is being cut. They say that at first by some dishonest method he earmarked for himself an undeservedly high pension, and that was not to someone's liking. Now from time to time Gulberdy receives these letters and so, swearing blue murder, he goes to the district council and comes back tired and grumpy as the devil. He cannot stand me, as if I write him these letters. But why am I here? My job is a little one: they send him a letter and I deliver it! But I always do this unwillingly. This time, too, I go round all the houses with an empty postbag to the very edge, to the house I detest in which there lives, on an allegedly undeserved pension, Gulberdy with his young wife, brought here from no-one-knows where.

Her name is Melike, she speaks in a manner which is unusual for our parts: sharp and lisping. When she tries to explain something to someone, in the corners of her mouth there often appears spittle which, however, never stops her from continuing the conversation. And although it's not nice for her, she likes to chatter and always tries to draw out her companion. On that account, perhaps, there was gossip concerning the *aksakal*'s young wife, and now Gulberdy won't let her step outside the house. He keeps her under lock and key, and when he goes to work in the field he never forgets to unchain the fierce dog, and he guards Melike even more jealously than his master.

Approaching the house, which, in contrast to the others, faced not the mountains but the desert, I was swearing no worse than Gulberdy himself, and he, on receiving letters from the district council, does this expertly. I did not wish to break in on the master, still less on his dog. The sun was blinding my eyes and burning my back. High Noon. On the street there were only the ants and I. Having a look to see there was no dog nearby, I entered the courtyard, with the bicycle's unoiled wheels creaking. Silence. Worrying. I stop by the veranda, and, holding onto a column supporting the roof of the veranda, I wait for old Gulberdy to rush out of the house, shaking his goat-like beard. A minute passes, then another, and there's no-one… I sound my bicycle bell and also pretend to clear my throat – kheh kheh! as if to say "Anyone there?" Not a sound… Leaning the bicycle against the steps, I wearily go up onto the terrace. I open the door – empty. I open another one – it's dark but you can see they've driven out the flies that morning and darkened the room with the blinds. I go through to the shed, draw back the curtain and – Oh Allah All-Merciful – what do I see? I've fallen into a trap! I leap out of the door before I am seized by the scruff of the neck and dragged off without cause or case to the executioner for coming at an untimely hour with a letter. I grab my bicycle by the 'horns' with hands gone suddenly sweaty from the agitation, I make haste to mount it and dash away as fast as can be. I look like mad in every direction – at the house, at the shed – in case old Gulberdy should rush out vicious as a dog and attack me.

Quick! Quick!

I rode out of the courtyard, I felt for the letter but it was not there – I looked back and there it was on the ground! I stopped. I stealthily looked about. Not a soul. Perhaps the old man was in the fields. If Gulberdy were at home he would have dashed out long ago. My heart began to ache sweetly: why not go back? Pick up the letter and while I'm there… just a little peek…

I can no longer control myself. I turn the bicycle around and head straight for the fateful door. Drawing back the curtain a little, I freeze. Melike, naked, stands in a trough, pouring bucket after bucket of water on herself. Stark naked! She wriggles like a snake as the cool water is poured on her shoulders and trickles in rivulets down her snow-white body, which is stealthily pawed now and again by rays of sunlight falling from somewhere above, through invisible crevices in the wooden roof of the shed. Her tensile young breasts quiver lightly and their pink little nipples are pointed straight at me. Just below her navel, like the fur of a yearling camel, one of the most mysterious places of the female body, glinting like gold, now as if deliberately showing under strips of light, now hiding shyly under the cascades of the hand-made waterfall, lures and seduces me. And all this lethal magnificence here – in a poky, dark shed! I stand there as if rooted to the spot, incapable of moving. But Melike just carries on enjoying her bath, as if she has not noticed me. It is lost in the debris of memory, I will never be able to say how much time passed like that. But this I do remember: Melike seems to freeze with the bucket raised above her head. Our eyes have met. It's time to bolt, but I cannot move from the spot, I haven't the strength. I just gaped, and she was not in the least mortified. On the contrary, handing me the bucket, she began making some seductive signs as if to say help me, you pour too! And the last thing I remember was her enticing white-toothed smile and the fine stream sweetly flowing between her pert breasts…

What followed remains for me a riddle to this day: suddenly some unknown force lifted me in the air together with my bicycle and hurled me far away from the object of my temptation.

I was in the street when I came to…

Daddy, of course, bought me a new bicycle, without asking superfluous questions. Gulberdy was silent too. But, by God, my sides, the back of my head and my soft place hurt for so long afterwards…

* * *

I awoke, my body exhausted with pain. In an attempt to remind them of me, in desperation I directed my gaze, full of suffering, at the women passing by – the doctor and the nurse; they noticed me and made a sign to say lie still for now, we will come to you, too, in a moment.

After a little while I saw them at my bed head.

"Another one's woken up!" said the nurse to the duty doctor. "Don't stir!" she warned me. "We're just going to take out the tube, you know, and you'll have to breathe independently!"

I made a movement of my eyes to say I understood, just get on with it!

Another two resuscitation doctors have approached, wearing pistachio-coloured coats, and stand at my bed head. I freeze in expectation. But why, oh why are they so slow, why don't they pull the tube out of my mouth, what are they waiting for? For me to suffocate? The movement of their hands is painfully slow, I can only guess that they are not so much preparing me, as preparing themselves for something. Then I see they are taking my face mask off but my mouth is still stuffed with something – I cannot make out what with, only it is impossible to breathe. Then, losing consciousness, I see someone pulling out of my mouth the partly blood-stained bandages holding the face mask, pulling and pulling them endlessly, like a conjurer drawing a garland out of a magic top-hat. And then – my first independent breath of air, like a potent narcotic, like a sweet poison. Collapsing into darkness, I hear the doctor's voice, apparently addressing the nurse:

"Careful! Don't damage the throat!"

And again – darkness and non-existence.

I realized that my situation was not one of the easiest, and non-existence could be my last place of refuge. Slowly but inexorably I was approaching it, darkness was enfolding me ever more tenderly and tightly, like a serpent its victim. I was sinking into a bottomless abyss, my body came out in a cold sweat and went numb. When the pain was gone, I guessed that here, now, at this prospect, soul and body will part ways. From this moment the soul is no longer sovereign of the body, it hovers in the stream of rising air, like a bird's feather lost in flight, and the bird herself flutters in her last irrational attempt, seized with mortal anguish. My sensations were doubled: my soul had flown away somewhere, indifferent to everything earthly, while my body in its last hope was clutching at the hands of the doctors of the resuscitation department, my saviours, unwilling eyewitnesses of my end. I realized that they were no longer able to help me, that my life was approaching its inevitable finale, its logical end. My body no longer reacted to life's impulses, it was fading fast, like firebrands falling into briny water coming under a squall of hurricane-force wind. I was going…

The only thing that did not want to die within me was some unruly part of my consciousness, where since childhood an indelible dream had settled, the delirium of my heart, created by me in my imagination – the image of my classmate Gozel, a carpet weaver, shapely as the stem of a *topalak*[3] of the steppes. I was going, but a tiny part of my brain, custodian of the image of my delicate big-eyed classmate, was fighting for my ravaged body with a power unknown to me. My brain did not want to depart into non-existence, did not wish to part from the bright world; it was desperately resisting the horrors of death, it was clinging to life, something in it was sparking up second by second and pushing me from the darkness of non-existence, trying time and again to re-unite my soul with my body. I my soul and I my body were struggling not to part, making agonizing efforts to gain unity with my first love, albeit darkened with the grief of loss. The solitary flower of the steppes trembled under the gusts of squally wind, reviving in my now other-world consciousness the features of Gozel, the girl from class nine, who had sorely wounded me in the past, refusing to read my love message which I had been writing with such trembling, and at no small risk to us both had contrived to pass to her at the end of Algebra class. But she not only refused to read the letter, she refused any reciprocity. "I'm getting married as soon as I leave school," she had said. "My boyfriend's parents insist on it." And now it was she who, having once rebuffed me, had now suddenly caught up with me at the gates of death and would not release me into the world of darkness. My soul, looking from somewhere outside at my body earmarked by death, wept and trembled like a helpless bee in the lethal embraces of a cruel black steppelands seven-stinged wasp. And in that instant, when several cells of my brain where the image of Gozel was kept declared their right to life, and the bitter aroma of her name was poured forth, that was when the last merciless skirmish between life and death began! I tossed and turned in delirium, I raved. The whole world rolled head-over-heels into the abyss, everything I had ever chanced to see even once – everything living and inanimate. Birds fell like a stone from the black horizon and, hitting the rocks, turned into disgusting soggy, shapeless lumps of flesh like rags. But the rocks themselves, black with brown tints, crumbled under these blows, and heavy, sharp fragments were falling on me. It was painful, as if I was being trampled underfoot, and at some other moment a bright yellow and blue light flashed on, but it was not salutary, above

---

3   Steppe plant with luxuriant inflorescence and slender stem.

my face there still swarmed flies, hideously large with wet sticky paws. In my ears a piercing wail sounded. My body remained under the rough heel of death, which relished its prowess, honed to repulsive perfection since the very first day of the origin of life. There was no salvation, I was defenceless, helpless before this cruel art of killing. No clock in the world will determine with appropriate accuracy how long this dragged on, while I flew, topsy-turvy, into a black pit, and then scrambled out, tearing my nails and biting my lips till they bled. Only a few days later, coming to myself, was I to realize with a feeble consciousness that, rescued from Hell, I had returned to this world, that death had retreated, and I had been granted some more time to live a while.

THE AMERICANS

I came to and saw I was lying in the centre of an L-shaped room by an antiquated high window generous of light and air. From the *fortochka* an autumnal freshness swept upon me. I saw the treatment trolley with medicines being wheeled towards me. Only ten or fifteen paces and the slanting rays of the morning sun separated me from the nurse in a light blue uniform and headscarf of the same colour. Together it all looked so angelically innocent: the sun, the branches of the trees, the rustling of variegated autumn leaves outside the window, but I already knew that any procedures would give me intolerable pain, and that the kindly nurse was my chief torturer. I roused up and braced myself, awaiting the start of the torments. Seconds began to split into still smaller moments, as the nurse implacably approached. She was almost alongside me, when suddenly the door of the ward opened and on the threshold appeared a group of strangers – tall, thick-set and stately. I was even able to discern the grey on the temples of some of them, so sharpened were all my sensations before the beginning of the unpleasant procedures.

The group was led by Podzolkov, also tall, and thin as a rake. He, as I learned later, had already managed to become head of the department in the time I had spent in resuscitation. Podzolkov started speaking, so softly that I could hardly make out his words, but the interpreter standing at his side enunciated each word clearly:

"Our Institute was founded in 1955."

The young man escorting the foreigners had quiet dark eyes and a straight nose without a bridge (a Greek perhaps? – I thought). As he translated Podzolkov's words from the Russian into English, he seemed for a time to embody him, so proud he was of what was said, and one got the impression that it was not his first year working at the Institute of Cardiovascular Surgery and, like all his colleagues, he was naturally involved in its successes.

"Or better to say we laid a cornerstone of our future success several years after that."

But while the interpreter was conveying his sentence to the foreigners who, I realized from their conversations, were Americans, Podzolkov looked expressively at the nurse and asked politely:

"Cover the medicines, please…"

But the nurse did not react. So Podzolkov, to avoid attracting the visitors' attention, repeated his request slightly more loudly:

"Yes, you… cover the medicines!"

Larisa, as the nurse was called, stared wide-eyed in fright, as if querying Podzolkov. Then the chief surgeon, speaking through his teeth, for the third time repeated his question, by now without much hope. At last the nurse understood the sense of what was said, and instantly covered the medicines with a snow-white cloth. I mentally thanked the doctor for his remark, because it was on the sterility of the medicines lying on the trolley that the life of post-operation patients depended – including mine.

But I realized how startled Larisa was by her own negligence from her cold fingers with which she fitfully grasped me by the shoulders. I heard the chattering of her teeth… No wonder she immediately committed the following negligence: she began stripping the bandage from my chest, which unsettled her boss still further, and now he exasperatedly hissed:

"Don't touch the bandage while the visitors are here…"

Then leaving in peace the nurse, who was numb with fright, Podzolkov rather hurriedly, as it seemed to me, began to usher his American colleagues from the resuscitation ward.

"It was Bakulev who paved this way," standing on the threshold of the ward, the interpreter almost rapped out the conclusion to the talk.

The Americans nodded in agreement, and one of them politely smiled at Podzolkov and said:

"He was very brave!"

When the glass door had closed behind the visitors, Larisa began to gradually come to her senses.

"The rotters dragged me in to replace Natasha!" she complained. I smiled wanly.

"Well, come on, get ready!" she continued. "Now we'll release you from the drainage. The abdominal cavity seems to be already in order."

The resuscitation doctor arrived, and she and the nurse together got down to work. First they worked on the post-operation suture. From the sharp, acrid smell of camphor and spirit of ammonia and the other procedures accompanying the bandaging, my strength was ebbing. But my main trial was still to come. The doctor, a thick-set woman in an apple-green blouse and trousers and a cap of the same hue, took hold of the tubes going under my ribs. Looking closely into my eyes, she tried to pull out one of the tubes. It felt as if something was coming out from under my heart. I bit my lips and felt their dry, bitter taste… It was so unpleasant that I evidently could not find apt expression to convey all my emotions. To endure the torture with dignity, I concentrated my gaze on the big drops of sweat forming right in front of my eyes on the broad forehead of the resuscitation doctor. I did not take my eyes off them and thought how incredibly hard it must be for a woman to perform such a job – causing pain to another. "Poor thing," I mentally pitied the doctor, looking at her embarrassed countenance. "What is it that's not going right for you? Have the tubes coalesced with my body?"

Continuing her desperate attempts, the doctor did not take her eyes off me either. At one point she asked in alarm:

"Does it not hurt? Why are you silent? Say something!"

I naturally wanted very much to support her, but my tongue got twisted, and what was there to say, anyhow? It hurt a lot, but the doctor herself must know that pretty well. Freeing me at last from the tubes, she wearily stroked my rough curls, and left.

With a glance I said goodbye to her and Larisa. They were already awaited by the next patient – the thick-set, shaven-headed man. My eyes closed of their own accord. But on hearing the thick bass, the swearing of my neighbour in the ward, I opened them again. The doctor's voice was heard instantly:

"It won't hurt, be patient! Be a tiny bit patient. Now, now. What's up? A strapping fellow like you hollering as if you're being cut to pieces. Look over there, at that skinny young man and how patient he was – not a sound!"

This praise from the lips of a woman I took as a well-deserved award and the most honourable of all the ones I had heard before. Later, as the resuscitation doctor and Larisa were passing me, I could not help saying, as my tongue had come to life again:

"Do you know who I am?" The unexpected clarity of my diction made them stop. "I'm a Turkmen!"

They smiled condescendingly, but I liked that too, and took their smiles as an unconditional acknowledgement of my qualities. And for the first time since the operation my mood improved since those little human weaknesses had become accessible to me.

Larisa, one step behind, somehow in her own way, almost conspiratorially, winked at me and again stuck her tongue out at me. And these secret signs, addressed only to me and no-one else, pleased me greatly!

… The next day I was transferred from the resuscitation unit to the ward. Apostolis had already prepared for discharge – his father was in a hurry to return to Athens. The young Greek left, leaving me his home address as he said goodbye, and the ward immediately went a bit dull. In no time it was turned into the most ordinary ward, without all those privileges – even the cleaning had now been handed over to the mummies here. The first to arrive was Gunta, a portly but at the same time surprisingly feminine Latvian woman. Normally in charge of the mop, she disclosed to me her grief at how unfairly they had dealt with the health of her four-year-old son Rainis, who suffered from a combined heart defect, the 'Fallot Tetrad'. The surgeons of the Institute could not decide to operate on the child owing to increased hypertension of the pulmonary artery. On learning that the Americans (the same ones who came with Podzolkov to the resuscitation ward) were planning to perform a demonstration operation for a highly complicated defect, Gunta obtained a consultation with them. The Americans examined her son and discovered that Rainis had, in addition to everything else, an inverted heart. But they had still agreed to operate on him. However, the Institute was insisting on the previously agreed programme. Gunta was not capable of understanding this, and she wept and wept. Twice a day she would come and clean my ward, which had become an individual one since the departure of Apostolis, and on each occasion the time-faded floor would be watered by her bitter tears.

So Gunta had to leave with her little son still untreated, receiving naught for her pains. Before her actual departure she came to see me, kissed me and said:

"Get well, please God, and don't dare to be ill again. God grant that (she said "that" with a soft Baltic accent) your heart may beat in time…" Her soft, moist lips again touched my cheeks.

From excitement and sympathy for her, my heart ached under my sternum, cut open and moved apart during the operation. Fastened with surgical silk and not having yet had time to knit together, my sternum throbbed softly and unpleasantly.

Subsequently my sternum was to cause me quite a bit more trouble. They were to pull from it, like a living vein, the threads tied in treble knots, and several days after that my temperature would begin to rise idiopathically… I was to flounder in delirium, and again the zinc coffin would loom up before my eyes, and I would dream of my broken-hearted father and brother accompanying my body imprisoned in a cold zinc shell. I would imagine a multitude of serious and trifling barriers erected on their path by petty officials with a taste for spurious order and greedy for lucre. These power-wielding punters would pop up before them here and there and, having got their bribe, disappear, leaving in their wake illegible signatures on documents resolving nothing. I would imagine that my father, genuinely heart broken, coming up at every step against depressing difficulties and unpredictable, outrageous extortion, might in the end dock his grief. The enormous sorrow and pain from the death of his son would be calmed, benumbed in his peasant heart knowing what his money would buy, long before my body is consigned to earth.

A few days later my terrible fantasy almost became reality. Mikhail Alexeyevich, the duty doctor who had stitched up my pericardium, connected the sternum and sewed up the fine muscles and skin, was so overcome with agitation at my idiopathic temperature that he would ask in a minute of desperation: "Have you any relatives in Moscow?" Then I would realize with horror that my situation was bad, that the end loomed ahead once more, for within the walls of the Institute I had learned plainly that idiopathic temperature was the commonest cause of death after an operation: it is a true sign that an infection has entered the heart! As a rule, such a patient is normally given just a few days of life after the fever has begun. To put it briefly – it is the beginning of the end!

But for now the tearful Gunta was leaning over me, kissing me with her lips moist with tears; and I am lying there, not daring to move, as under my skin the fine muscles of the not yet knitted bones of my sternum are trembling.

"Goodbye, my darling! Get well soon. So we'll be going back like that – doomed… Oh God, when will my torments be finished?"

"A fine lot those Americans!" I tried to console Gunta. "Will their hands drop off if they do one extra operation?"

Would you think this operation would cost them more? Better to transplant hearts than all those presidents!"

But Gunta was not soothed by my tirade, as she was now thinking only about her ill-fated Rainis. And I realized that being doomed was the greatest misfortune. There were a few in the Institute like Rainis, they all dreamed of suffering any torments to get better. To those who just could not reach the operating table which offered the hope of life, even the post-operation pains and sufferings of others seemed the height of a felicity which, alas, was not accessible to everyone.

After saying goodbye to Gunta, I fell to daydreaming – about my home; about the fact that I would soon be returning to my family healthy, perhaps even healthier than I was before the Institute. I was dreaming that any moment now when I looked at the door it would open and Mary would enter the ward…

A BOUQUET FROM
NESKUCHNY GARDENS

The first thing I saw on coming to, after the stupefying but painkilling injections I had been stuffed with in resuscitation, was a luxuriant bouquet of leaves. What a miscellany of hues there were – crimson and reddish-purple, orange and rich yellow, and also green, only lightly touched by the flame of autumn – well, just unrivalled beauty!

This wondrous gift was presented to me by Mary, breaking the silence of the ward with her little sing-song silver voice:

"Come to? Hey, breathe in nature!"

The bouquet truly exhaled the aroma of Neskuchny Gardens, for it had absorbed the smell of their soil, the bark and leaves of the trees, the taste of the diamond drops. The bouquet was admired by all who came to congratulate me on a successful operation.

"Why is your name not Russian?" I asked Mary, when we were left alone. "You're a Muscovite, surely?"

"Because Grandmother was French," she replied.

"But Mary, if I am not mistaken, is an English name. How does Lord Byron put it?

> "Hills of Annesley, bleak and barren,
> Where my thoughtless childhood stray'd,
> How the northern tempests, warring,
> Howl above thy tufted shade!
>
> "Now no more, the hours beguiling,
> Former favourite haunts I see;
> Now no more my Mary smiling
> Makes ye seem a heaven to me."

She saddened a little, her face took on a faint blush and, lowering her head, she sat in silence for several moments. Then, with her accustomed ease, she was instantly transformed: she smiled broadly, moved forward and, of a sudden, unexpectedly placed her hand on mine.

"Don't let's talk about that..." Mary looked at me with a surprisingly open expression, so that I felt very slightly at a loss. And she leaned her classical little head so the golden threads of her hair lay with their ends on my pillow, right by my face. For the first time since the operation there penetrated my still not fully recovered lungs the tender aroma of a young female body. This still further excited my weak heart, which gave notice of itself with a sudden piercing pain.

"You tell me how everything went there. Of course, I already know everything about the operation, but I would like you to tell me too. What is it like?"

Mary's eyes shone with a kindly light and her resonant teenager voice awoke contradictory feelings in me.

"Well, how..." I tried to keep cool and overcome the excitement which the proximity of this skinny little girl with the silvery voice had stirred in me. "It's all very simple. First they saw open the sternum, prize it apart, from above and below they fix iron spreaders, sort of rods, that's all. The rest is plain sailing: they just fumble a bit in the heart and darn it somewhere..."

Mary laughed loudly at my yarn and stroked my hand.

"A likely story! How can you darn a heart?"

"Well, patch it. Will that do?"

"A heart isn't a sock to be darned. You need the finest jeweller's craft, don't you?"

"Well, not quite jeweller's craft," I pronounced sadly, remembering certain details which accompanied the actual operation.

But Mary would not let me plunge into my sad memories.

"Nazarli, I don't think there is anyone luckier than you in the world, yet you're down in the dumps. How can that be?"

"No, it can't!" I agreed, and changed the subject. "But you explain to me why Grandmother gave you an English name. Where was her French pride?"

Mary smiled, revealing tiny teeth like pomegranate seeds.

"That secret is lost in the past. Granny died fifteen years ago. Now no-one will ever know why she acted so unpatriotically."

"May the Kingdom of Heaven be hers!" said I and then asked: "Mary, help me to be convinced that I am in this world, there's something missing for me to be totally sure. Incidentally, I had hopes of meeting your Grandmother there…"

"All the same, you preferred to stay with her grand-daughter!" she joked and, smiling, reached for the bouquet, which lay on the night table. "Doesn't my presence convince you? What will convince you? A kiss, perhaps?"

"Why ever not? We're alone…" I ventured.

But instead of the expected kiss I was granted the aroma of autumn leaves presented to my face. This time they smelled of swallows' nests. For a moment I imagined myself climbing a ladder. Reaching the very highest rung, I stretch up and smell the swallows' nest, delighting in the consummate skill of the mysterious birds so dear to my heart, their spherical home, by some miraculous means fastened to a beam on the veranda. I see myself then with all my might dragging the ladder from the scene of the 'crime' before Mummy catches me at my illicit occupation. I buried my nose in the bouquet and inhaled the smell of the leaves deeper – wonderful! My lungs did not resist, I did not even cough.

"Mary, where did you find such marvellous leaves?" I asked.

"In Neskuchny Gardens. Leaves like that can only be found there. You know, they say Pushkin himself liked to walk there. It's an age-old garden from back in the eighteenth century! I'm wondering… Didn't Pushkin pick leaves there for his Natalya?"

"Could be," I responded. "As soon as I start walking I will work on that. By then I hope you will have actually had your operation."

Mary bent her head really low. She was silent and I was silent too, not knowing the reason for this sudden grief. Then she gave a deep sigh and said:

"It looks as if they don't want to perform the operation… I don't know if something suspicious is going on, they keep delaying it."

"But you've already had the tests!"

"Yes, and I've had the sounding. It was just after that something inexplicable started. I don't know… Tomorrow my parents are meeting the director, it may become clearer, we'll see." She shook her little head and smiled: "Come on, Nazarli, we won't talk about that! Today I want to enjoy myself together with you."

Unexpectedly, she leaned over me and pressed her fine, tender lips to mine for a little while.

"Could I call you thou?"

"Of course," I gasped, feeling the taste of her hot lips, involuntarily regretting that the kiss was so brief.

"Have pity on me," I whispered. "My heart is about to burst."

"With fear?" Mary asked, giving me an artful look. "Are you afraid someone will peek?" Now the expression of her eyes changed. The artfulness was suddenly mingled with grief. I too was involuntarily embarrassed. Perhaps she had already heard of my fleeting encounters with the young nurse, although she had only been at the Institute for a few days. So striking had been the disparity between her joke and her look.

But perhaps her grief was for a completely different reason. I felt there lay an invisible barrier between us – I had already stepped into the future, while Mary still remained in the past, standing before a closed door to the unknown.

Mary stood up and started saying goodbye. I said I would wait for her all the time and the others could go to Hell! I did not want to see anyone or anything! She smiled and nodded. I was soon convinced that Mary took my words seriously. She came to see me more and more often and audaciously. The ones she was wary of were Babka Nastya and Olga (my) Nikanorovna, albeit the latter, of course, had done her no harm and apparently did not intend to. Clearly, Olga understood better than anyone the innocence of my relationship with Mary – I could not even get out of bed independently. That might well have been in the nurse's eyes a guarantee of the chastity of our friendship.

But the more often we met, the more alarming the situation became. It was evident that my relationship with Mary was acquiring ever more sensual undertones. I could no longer go without her for even an hour, and she would come into my ward as if into our shared home…

Of course, there was strong justification for such frequent visits – she was regarded as a sister of mercy: she brought me water, straightened the blankets, opened the *fortochka* in the mornings – on the whole, there was always enough for her to do. Mary would leave my ward only at the time when Father came or our friend the elderly Yulia Alexandrovna visited me and brought parcels. Mary and I would be forced to part most unwillingly even for a short time. But even when we were alone together I constantly felt her concern: Mary would glance at the door now and again, shivering at every rustle, at the soft sound of footsteps along the corridor. And once that which was bound to happen sooner or later did occur: through the golden gossamer of Mary's hair as she leaned over me in a kiss, I saw in the doorway of the ward Olga (my) Nikanorovna… Her big hazel eyes scrutinized us with curiosity, with a spot of mockery: "Well, my little love-birds, caught at it?" For a while we were all in a state of paralysis, speechless. The first to come to her senses was Olga (my) Nikanorovna. She hung a clean towel on the back of the bed and, looking me reproachfully straight in the eye, shook her head. Then she would repeat this movement of hers every time our eyes met, if only for an instant. She was bound to shake her head. With a touch of sadness in her eyes.

However, after that incident Mary and I had hardly anyone to fear, and she would be with me for whole days, except for certain hours. But this happy madness did not last long. Soon my condition began to deteriorate rapidly: the aroma of fresh bouquets from Neskuchny Gardens which Mary brought daily and her silver whisper would float to me as if from afar, and I could barely make out her words, being in the grip of a high temperature which kept rising and rising… The doctors took turns, seeing me now one at a time, now in a group, but they could not understand the reason for my high fever, and then it became clear that my temperature was idiopathic…

THE LAST NIGHT

I had at the very most several days left to live. But by this time I had already assimilated the new form of my existence, i.e. the endless teetering between life and death, so I met the next twist in the skirmish with death without any special fuss. There can hardly be many people who have undergone the same sort of trial and managed to survive, and their borderline condition would hardly have been as prolonged and hopeless as mine. But if there are, they are undoubtedly people of a special destiny with invaluable experience, and each one of them is entitled to enrich the book of human existence with his own page about his acute sense of the fragility of life, to warn others against too much recklessness.

Despite all the efforts of the doctors and nurses, my temperature, which was wearing me out, was stubbornly creeping up and seemed to be finally finishing off my being. And then I comprehended with horror that the approaching night could turn out to be the last in my young life.

"Forty…" the duty doctor was thus curtly briefed by the nurse, and the black ripe plums of her eyes were embedded in the dying embers of my memory.

"Give him the injection!" cried Mikhail Alexeyevich under his breath, as he held my pulse.

I felt the cold sting of the needle and nothing more.

My body shrank, reacting to contact more by instinct than anything. That is all that remained in my memory of the procedure, I no longer felt either pain or relief. My consciousness faded, having managed to glimpse the last frame: them starting to tear my clothing off.

Later, regaining consciousness, I saw that I was lying almost stark naked on a white sheet, and a large lop-eared fan was earnestly waving its vanes above me, in an attempt to drive the fever from me. Mikhail Alexeyevich still stood by my side. Seeing I had opened my eyes, he asked:

"Have you anyone in Moscow? Any family?"

I did not manage to answer him immediately. I tried to raise my head, but the task proved too hard, beyond my powers.

"Father is here," I groaned. "Why?"

"No matter…" Mikhail Alexandrovich muttered. "I just…"

"I was asked that yesterday, the duty doctor asked."

"Sorry, I didn't know," he patted me on the shoulder reassuringly. I clearly felt the cold of his big hand.

A pain shot through me, I wanted to burst into tears. I felt something was wrong and realized they were saying farewell to me. I began to watchfully follow the movements of the doctor who continued to examine me. I became breathless, I twitched, signalling that I felt bad. Mikhail Alexandrovich placed an oxygen mask on my face and turned on a tap on the tube above my bed.

"Breathe deeper! Deeper breaths!"

Tamara came and they began to talk quietly together. They said more with their eyes. I watched them and what was going on around me. Out of the corner of my eye I could see preparations of some kind. Tamara was working impassively: in her gauze mask she looked strict; clearly, not for nothing was she considered the meanest in the department. But her eyes were not mean, they were even beautiful… But for those awaiting an operation there was a lack of kindness in them, and that was the same as looking mean as a shrew.

The door of the next ward creaked, the sound of footsteps was heard, and when the door opened we all saw Lida.

"What's happened?" she asked, poking her head into the ward.

Mikhail Alexeyevich glanced at her disapprovingly over his spectacles and said drily:

"Nothing special. Go to bed!"

The door closed. The nurse started removing the bandage from my chest, repeating:

"You must trust me! I bandaged it only last night. I did everything properly!"

The doctor inspected the suture carefully, felt it with his finger here and there, pretending not to hear the nurse's grumbles.

"Bandage it up!" he said, finishing the inspection. "Everything's fine, unfortunately… I cannot see anything, the suture seems to be in order."

I listened intently to their conversation. And soon I felt the rhythm of my breathing disrupted. Something was pressing on my heart, and this "something" was hampering my breathing, which had become intermittent, as if tottering and stumbling.

"Breathe deeper!" said Mikhail Alexeyevich to me.

But I was breathing deep as it was, with all my might, but of course before death you cannot catch your breath.

Finally downcast, Mikhail Alexeyevich ordered the nurse:

"Quick, bring the test tubes and hypodermic for a blood sample!"

Tamara went towards the exit, but at the same time again displayed dissatisfaction, as if to say she would not tolerate the dictatorial tone or something else of the kind.

"Bimbo!" cried Mikhail Alexeyevich after her in a fit of temper. "Bring them means bring them! We need to take an urgent blood test, do you understand or not?"

I started shivering and the doctor covered me with a sheet.

But a cold gloom was rapidly enfolding me all over, from feet to head, was chasing at my heels and soon overtook me completely in a pit of icy water. I was either asleep or unconscious, but suddenly came to and had an unexpected feeling of suffocation. When, with the utmost effort, I raised my heavy eyelids and opened my eyes, I discovered with horror that there was no-one by me. And I thought for a moment – have I really died? Perhaps I'm in the other world!

Something cold struck my cheek, it was my saviour - the oxygen mask, which had fallen off my face. It was lying still on my pillow next to me, and I immediately fell on it. I gasped – quickly, greedily, gradually plunging into a miry, hollow silence, to awaken in the person of a youth of the Goat Clan slain in his innocence by foes, to bear upon himself just once all the futility of death, to answer for someone else's sins and carry someone else's cross without being a prophet.

REVENGE OF THE FOXES

A day of blinding sunshine… It takes a while for the brightness around me to gel, take on three dimensions, solidity and shapes enough for me to see the desert spread out in all directions as far as the horizon, the flock of sheep agitated by something, steep-browed wolfhounds lying nearby raising their heavy heads, perplexed at what is happening around them, and also three horsemen – right in front of me. They have galloped up silently or have appeared from under the ground, but whatever the case I have been taken by surprise: I have had no time to either hide or prepare for their appearance. The horsemen are unhurriedly honing their sabres, eyeing me in contempt and performing some ritual, looking around furtively, as if wondering if there is someone nearby who could interfere and prevent them.

I am an unarmed teenager, doomed, standing before my predators, guilty only of belonging to the Goat Clan. I belong against my own will, through an unfortunate chain of events: my parents, my father and my mother, man and wife, who conceived me – they are from the Goat Clan, a clan which long before their birth and mine managed to quarrel with the Fox Clan. These three looming above me are warriors of the Fox Clan.

For how many years, how many decades have these two clans been fighting, pursuing and killing each other? For what reason? The hostility may have started over pastures, the cause may have been an insult inflicted by one of my volatile ancestors on a person from the Fox Clan. Today there are few who know about this, it is of no interest to anyone – why should it be if it is just a matter of how many heads have been cut off? The reason is erased from the memory and forgotten – but not the insult. Therefore the blood feud continues and will never die out. How many real men have been cut down! How many of them have been killed in merciless clashes! How many have been slain by stealth, after being tracked down and ambushed, like me! How many?

The first to be killed are the boldest, in open, honourable combat, then anyone deft with the sabre, and after them comes the turn of those with a masculine name. Be he strong or weak, bold or not – no matter: if he wears a *papakha* on his head – that means he is a man, and if he himself is not able to fight, he will spawn brats, and they… In vain will women of both hostile clans dress their boys as girls, hide them a little distance from the malign eyes of young men: all the same their sons are doomed. Common malice, growing day by day, becomes a cause of murder and every decapitated head is a fresh curse for both clans, the Goat Clan and the Fox Clan.

There were no fewer brave *batyrs* in our clan than in the Fox Clan, only our warriors were unlucky – the brave were the first to be cut down, at the very start of the enmity, then came the turn of the others, then the cowards were butchered too. Thus all the men were killed.

I am the last man of the Goat Clan. I am fifteen years old, it's just the time to kill me, because I well remember the milk that nourished me, and have long been secretly playing with a sabre from a shepherd! Warriors from the Fox Clan tracked me down in time, they know that if they don't exterminate me now, I myself will be killing soon. (That is what they are thinking. I can read it in their eyes, and I don't expect mercy.) The sword of death hangs over me. Soon my head will roll beneath the feet of my predators, I will pay with it for the hot-headedness of some nameless ancestor of mine whom I have never seen, because he long ago paid with his blood for the deed and also went the way of his own victim. So it is for me to answer for others' sins, to be the last to answer…

I cry out in a frenzy, but cannot hear my own voice, I weep bitter tears, but they stay inside me, my eyes are dry, and the enemy squint at me, sharpening their sabres. They have no wish to understand that I do not want to die, because I am too young and have only just discovered for myself all the enchanting beauty of the mountains and desert, and the heavens above me, be they bright with the sun or with golden stars. And have they galloped up here to rob me of all this? I am the last man of the Goat Clan. I grew, melded with the quiet of the vast desert, and have only just begun to understand the language of the animals – timid hares and bloodthirsty wolves, insatiable cowardly jackals and *zeren* with their virgin eyes like hers I met in a camp of herders coming down to us from nearby mountains for the spring festival. If only they knew I had only just seen real life in the mysterious figure of her who dawned on my soul with her shy smile. A girl who, giving me an heir, could immortalize both me and our clan!

But the predators, planning to kill me, with a blank impassiveness raise their hands to the heavens and whisper prayers of some kind: they're asking the Almighty to spare them and their descendants and protect them from the hostile sabre. I do not think Allah will hear them, will forgive and not punish them for such a heinous crime. Surely I am not guilty of anything towards them. I have not killed anyone, although mother did nourish me with the milk of vengeance to the cradle songs of son avenging father, killed before he was born. I never ever saw father – our enemies saw to that, those people from the Fox Clan. Altogether I saw few people around, because I was hidden in the desert, where I was to become a warrior and avenge my clan, my father, the tears of my young widowed mother. And only once, recently at night I was taken to the village to show and delight relatives – the last man of the Goat Clan had grown up for vengeance.

It was the first time I had seen my village and that only one who, unnoticed by the others, bestowed on me a special glance, and in that youthful beauty I immediately recognised her who would perpetuate our stricken clan. Through the lattice of the *kibitka* cart where I had been hidden from strangers' eyes, I spent the livelong day with trembling heart cherishing her easy gait and hearing the tinkle of silver frills woven into her four plaits. She walked barely touching the ground, as if she knew her body was a precious vessel housing immortality.

Was that vessel now really doomed to remain empty just because a curved sabre knew no mercy?

Oh, oh, curved sabres, how many heads you've cut off, how many woes you have brought upon people – both your own and others! Whetted against your opponent's sabres, you washed the enemy in blood, but the enemy only? Didn't you first bathe in the blood of your own clan? Lest the steel be blunted on the enemies' necks, it is first tempered in the blood of your own people – this should be remembered by anyone who has drawn his curved sabre from the scabbard! It is impossible to subdue other clans without having subdued your own, to bring others to their knees without crushing your own people, and any war is fratricidal. And now my blood brothers are preparing to kill me. I stand doomed, my strength is ebbing, and my lips against my own will begin to pray for mercy:

"Agam, agam-jan! Don't kill me! I haven't done anything bad – don't kill!"

"It's a good thing you haven't…" one of the horsemen sneers. "That means you haven't managed to yet. And why should you burden your soul with a sin – do something bad? Be glad your conscience will remain unsullied, you'll fly like a white bird straight to paradise! And in paradise there must be many good people, you'll get on fine there, and the main thing is you won't have to hide any more, or run after the flock in the summer heatwave – the *jowza* or the freezing cold of winter – the *chille*… Believe me, that's not the worst thing that can await a person, son, there are worse things…"

"Yes, I know there are worse, but all the same don't kill me! If you kill me then I won't see anyone or anything. And no-one will see me."

"Who's planning to kill you, silly?" says another one soothingly, but he himself is sharpening his sabre. His voice is tender, so tender that my blood goes cold in my veins from fear. "Silly little chap, where did you get the idea that we're planning to kill you? Just turn and face Mecca! Go on, in the direction of the Kaaba, there's a clever boy…"

I dare not disobey, and humbly face that direction, looking where shepherd Dortkuli-aga – our distant relative – prays five times a day. Just today, before leaving for the village to get groceries, he faced that way and said a *namaz* at dawn. He went, and I was left on my own with the flock. And now I clearly hear behind my back the mechanical heart beat of the warriors of the Fox Clan, growing stronger every moment.

The horsemen finish praying and I hear behind my back the "Amin!" in unison. And then I have time to sense with the back of my head the murder weapon pitiably, softly whining as it slices the air… The curved sabre of the warrior from the Fox Clan descended on my neck so swiftly that my eyelids had no time to close…

And now, already dead, with a glance of my now sightless eyes I pray the enemies to bury my decapitated body and not leave it to be torn to pieces by wild animals. I implore them to bury me in Muslim fashion, and not let the steppeland birds of prey peck out my eyes. But the horsemen neither hear nor see my prayer, they leave hurriedly, stealthily. They gallop away…

I never managed to do anything good or bad in this world; I grew up in eternal mourning: I was suckled on the milk of vengeance, fell asleep to a lullaby that was more like a war song, and once only, almost furtively, saw her who could have given me immortality, the girl whose hair was twisted into four plaits. I had looked at her so shyly that she must have hardly sensed my young glance. And here I am falling dead on the scorched sand, and my head is rolling on the ground after my enemies, after my murderers with just one entreaty: bury me!

But the people from the Fox Clan do not hear, they gallop away… And in my ears there resounds for the last time either the drumming of hooves or the mechanical beat of the hearts of the merciless perpetrators of someone else's ill will. My murderers gallop away from my lifeless body to continue on this earth their cruel trade in endless ways. No, the sabre is not a scalpel, I whisper in my febrile delirium, returning from the non-existence subduing my consciousness to the realities of the hospital…

MY LANGUAGE IS MY ENEMY

The suture on my chest broke on the third day after the beginning of the crisis, and only then did my idiopathic temperature at last begin to fall. The doctors sighed with relief: thank God the heart is clear and the infection is superficial, so we won't lose the lad, we'll be able to pull him through…

Without delay I was transferred to the dressing ward, where they started to pull out the rotted threads, and there were more than enough of them: during the operation they sewed the suture on the sternum in three layers, tying each surgical suture with knots. Now they were pulling them out of my chest one by one, like veins.

From the dressing ward, to my great distress, I did not land back in my own apartments, the trolley was wheeled straight to the 'rotteds' ward. It was a five-bed ward, with the beds standing close together. The passage between them was so narrow that the doctor or nurse, bending over one patient, were almost resting their bottoms on the faces of the others, lying opposite.

On the first day, on the way from the dressing ward, Semyon Arkadyevich and Suzanna Temirovna were conversing quietly as they slowly pushed the trolley, on which I lay with eyes closed, worn out by the harrowing procedure.

"It's a good thing that it's outside, but, Suzanna Temirovna…" Semyon Arkadyevich was saying barely audibly. "But what if it had got into the abdominal cavity? No, thank God, the lad's been lucky. I was thinking the worst…"

"How could you help thinking it, Semyon Arkadyevich?" Suzanna Temirovna said just as quietly. "Just yesterday and the day before…"

I lay there and listened to their conversation at one remove, as if they were not talking about me, but someone else separate from me. It was difficult for me myself to believe that the most dreadful thing was already behind me, that the mortal danger hanging over me in the past few days, like a Sword of Damocles, had passed. I lay there, enjoying my black humour: "How lucky during the operation the infection pierced my suture, not my heart!" At that time I did not know how long I would have to languish in the cramped and stuffy ward of the 'rotteds', what torments and setbacks I would have to suffer. I had already become a kinsman of physical pain, it was comprehensible to me, I was acquainted with it. But how could I foresee that still greater shocks awaited me, just as the usual physical pain was to start to give way, receding day by day?

Soon after I had been placed in the ward of the 'rotteds', which, incidentally, was located directly opposite the historic ward No 6, where my institute Odyssey began, Nurse Rita came and brought me the news:

"Did you know Mary is being accepted for the operation? The list is out already."

"Is today Monday or Tuesday?" I asked Rita, not yet strong enough to be joyful about anything.

"Today is Friday already!" Rita replied, drawing out the words, and in her wide-open blue-grey eyes I noticed a slight pity. "Oh dear, have you lost count of the time?" she asked, shaking her head. Her freshly washed chestnut coloured hair shone and smelled of fragrant shampoo.

"So it's Friday." I answered feebly. "That's fine... And what is Mary doing?"

"Obviously, she's delighted! I promised to help her prepare for the operation, and she'll be taken on my shift."

"No need to coddle her! She's a healthy lass, can't she do it herself?" Anatoli Yakovlevich, my neighbour on the left, butted into our conversation. "Mary's already sixteen, isn't she, or not?"

"Seventeen!" replied Rita with obvious reluctance. "That's not the point..."

"What is then?" asked Anatoli Yakovlevich, sitting up with the help of bands attached to the back of the bed ('reins' as they called them at the Institute), and he prepared to discuss the problem thoroughly.

But Rita displayed no wish to continue the discussion: pleading urgent work, she left, leaving me a handful of tablets. Rita's reluctance to maintain the conversation and her hasty departure put me slightly on my guard.

Soon I was visited by my friends in adversity, our whole company led by Mary. She had really brightened up. When the guys had left, Mary delayed, she could not wait to discuss with me the news of the operation being prepared for. A pity we could not talk in secret together – Anatoli Yakovlevich watched us continually and tried to start a general conversation. Mary left disappointed.

Apart from me and Anatoli Yakovlevich, there were in the ward: a twelve-year-old boy from Georgia – Bezhan, his peer Dima and another, Dmitri, who looked about twenty. Under the watchful eye of Anatoliy Yakovlevich, Dmitri spent whole days reading a tattered volume two bricks thick.

"Read, Dmitri, read!" Anatoli would keep prompting him whenever he noticed he was going to set the book aside. "Then you hand it to Nazarli. A good book," he added, now addressing me. "It's called *The Incendiaries*. It's all true. Some people now want to forget, but we need to remember everything, nothing should be forgotten. Just take a look at that," he said, taking a newspaper from the bedside table. "You know what they're doing? They've hung the Israeli flag out of the window and declared a hunger strike, the swine – they're not being allowed to go to the West, you see! They've gorged themselves here, and now they want out! They don't like it in our country! Swine, damned dissidents… Their kind should be shot!"

Holding my chest, I turned to look at my neighbour. Anatoli Yakovlevich was really upset and angry, as if they had hung the Israeli flag out of the window of his flat. He chucked the newspaper on the bedside table and started to slowly sink onto the pillow.

"Did you hear that?" he asked me when he had lain down.

"No," I replied, "I've learnt it from you."

"No, I don't mean that, I mean the whistling, did you hear it? Squelch! A sound like that when I lie down or get up. A cleft, infection! It'll never heal. If it weren't for that I would have signed out last week." And returning to the previous subject, he added: "And with them, I realize, there should be short shrift! All the danger is from them! So there's no point in indulging them!"

"If the danger is from them, wouldn't it be better to let them go before they do any harm?"

My careful remark upset Anatoli Yakovlevich even more than the report in the paper. He burst into an angry tirade:

"Swine! Traitors! Shoot them – full stop! What's the point of messing about with them? They want us to let them go abroad and get all those jeans... The rotters weren't unmasked in time! They plundered us, now they're soaping themselves over there. And then, just you see, they'll be asking to come back!"

"But they're not all leaving," said Dima senior. "It's only those who have somewhere to go, those who want to see the world..."

"That's it!" responded Anatoli Yakovlevich, livening up. "Now they'll all leave. We've got to let them see a bit more of the world! But tell me, why didn't they leave before?"

"Before when?" I inquired.

"When? When they went without trousers with bare bottoms!"

"We Turkmens have a saying: 'Even to beg you need possessions!'"

"All the same they're swine! They're all traitors!"

"You cannot treat them all the same?"

"You can't? Why's that? Swine and espionage agents, there's no question about it! But do you want them to auction everything off? Think hard before you defend traitors!"

"Let's assume I don't defend them. Treason in our country is considered the most despicable deed. In the last century, when the Russians conquered Turkmenia, they very much wanted to find a traitor among the Turkmens who would help seize Geok-Tepe. They searched but could not find one! A Russian officer later wrote in his diary that the Turkmens had absolutely no understanding of what it meant to betray one's Motherland, one's brothers. That was how it used to be, when the people did not know slavery."

"So you're exalting these...? So where is your patriotism?" my opponent exclaimed, his voice breaking with agitation.

"I'm not exalting them, I'm trying to understand why they are leaving. And my convictions, incidentally, are irrelevant here. Patriotism has its varieties, too. You've no doubt heard of the State variety, Anatoli Yakovlevich, eh?"

My neighbour's face changed. His cheeks, pink with an even glow even after the operation, suddenly paled. Grabbing the 'reins', he pulled himself up, sat up on the bed, and, scowling with pain, said angrily but at the same time with grief in his voice:

"You don't understand! Call me what you like but I… I…" Anatoli Yakovlevich pitifully beat his breast with his fist. "I am, you see, a patriot, I am in pain for our State, our _Derzhava_!"

"Anatoli Yakovlevich, patriotism and love of _Derzhava_ are, incidentally, two different things. _Derzhava_ comes from the word _derzhat,_ to hold! And is it bad if a person sees different countries? It does not stop a person who loves his Motherland from loving her still more. Wasn't Miklukho-Maklay a patriot? I'm really saying you cannot be forced to be good. Why was it that before the Revolution you could travel wherever you wished, but now – don't even dare to think of it? I might also want to do like Miklukho-Maklay."

"Now is not the time, you'll have to wait. Everything will settle down, it'll sort itself out, then maybe…" Anatoli Yakovlevich was now talking calmly but as unkindly as before. He was obviously not happy that instead of talking about traitors he was having to discuss a subject which was extremely ticklish in his view. "I tell you, now is not the time to go scrambling abroad."

"But you only have one life! How long can you wait? And when it is all sorted out there's still no end in sight!"

"Don't try to be clever. People used to be stood against the wall for that kind of talk. And now you lie there and argue… Everyone's got too clever!"

From the pressure of 'patriotism' I felt my sternum starting to go up and down nastily and my heart seemed to have been left without any protection, like in the open air. Even my skin hurt, tightly drawn with wide sticking plaster criss-crossing the wound. With some bewilderment, I peered into Anatoli Yakovlevich's eyes, into their surprising sky-blueness. And I could not understand if those eyes belonged to a living person…

I could not help myself:

"So you'd like them to be shot? The methods of execution vary, it's not necessarily a bullet in the forehead. It can be on the quiet like in the NKVD…"

But Anatoli Yakovlevich arrogantly ignored my words, and that day each of us stayed with his own opinion. But this dispute of ours would not come to an end, it would flare up from time to time. The discussion broke out with renewed force several days later, on Tuesday, I think, yes! – the same day when Mary again had her operation postponed…

* * *

On that day I was in a terrible mood. Mary had just run out of my ward all in tears. She was grief-stricken and I had spent a long time trying to reassure her and give her hope, for which purpose I had thought up some stupid explanations for what had happened. But my words had been unconvincing. However, not being able to find any sound reasons for the operation being refused, I could not keep silent, and so I kept trying to reassure her, but the girl at length flew into a rage both at me and the whole wide world, and ran away sobbing.

At length, disconcerted, I lay, looking at the ceiling, and almost failed to hear what was going on around me. I reproached myself for being no little to blame, as I simply had not been able to find just the words which were vitally necessary for my dear Mary. Evidently, in the heat of my feelings something very important had evaded me, something which would have given her hope for the future. How could I know that desperation would penetrate so deeply into her tender soul, that tragedy was already on the doorstep…

I was totally plunged into my own thoughts, thinking of Mary's situation over and over again, and for a long time I was unable to return to reality, to the ward. I was withdrawn from my torpor by a loud voice: it was Anatoli Yakovlevich, who had spent ages lecturing Bezhan irksomely about something, and now angrily cried:

"You must learn the language properly! Otherwise you won't know zilch!"

Bezhan, gaping in fright, looked at me in confusion, seeking support. I naturally had no wish to run up against the rudeness of my neighbour, who, as I already knew, was not accustomed to hearing out someone else's opinion, let alone respecting it. Nevertheless, I was obliged to stand up for the dispirited boy.

"How have you decided, Anatoli Yakovlevich, that he has learned the language badly? What, have you been holding his exercise book marked 'poor' in your hands?"

"But he doesn't understand a word!" Anatoli Yakovlevich said in surprise. "To whatever you ask he stays silent! He hasn't a clue…"

"But you could ask him in Georgian," I advised.

"Come off it, Nazarli! How am I to know Georgian?"

"So what do you want of him?" I responded by raising my voice too, not without satisfaction observing that, for the first time since we had been neighbours, on Anatoli Yakovlevich's face the habitual self confidence was briefly replaced by a pitiable embarrassment. "And it turns out you yourself haven't a clue," I said.

But his consternation did not last long, and soon, forgetting about Bezhan, he turned to me and started lecturing me:

"No, my dear fellow, don't try and scare me! I wasn't asking him in Chinese, was I? In Russian! Russian is…" In his indignation Anatoli Yakovlevich could not immediately find the right word. "A great language, you know! Ah, I expect you're being quirky on purpose. I was recently on a work trip to Estonia, and there they also all speak among themselves not in our language – it's some kind of mockery. It's not right! They teach you for so many years and all in vain!" Anatoli Yakovlevich waved his hand in annoyance.

He was not the first person I had heard this kind of argument from, and I knew that any riposte was useless, and more often than not taken as undermining internationalism which, as far as language is concerned, is highly regarded by all Soviet patriots. Any other time I probably would not have continued the dispute, but by now I was quite riled by Anatoli Yakovlevich's self-confidence.

"All in vain, you say? So rather than teach those who don't want to learn Russian, why not learn their language?"

"What use is Georgian to me? I'm not going to live there!"

"But Bezhan is soon going home to his Motherland, where he can speak whatever he likes, be it Georgian, be it Abkhazian or Ossetian – that's his business. He may not have any use for the Russian that is forcibly instilled in him."

"What's that – no use? Do you realize what you're saying? Russian is Great Lenin's language!" Anatoli Yakovlevich declared with passionate pride in the creator of the Soviet multinational state.

"So what?" said I, mentally cursing myself for getting into such an undignified dispute. "And Georgian is the language of the Great Shota Rustaveli! And Turkmen is the language of the Great Makhtumkuli!"

"Oh no!" cried Anatoli Yakovlevich. "You tell me in which language they made the Revolution!"

"They made it in various ones! The Russians made it in Russian, the Georgians in Georgian!" I burst out in reply, trying not to give way to my neighbour even in shouting. I did, however, take the precaution of holding my chest where, under the sticking plaster, bandages and thin skin, the still unjoined bones of my sternum moved scarily – it was still less than half a month since the operation.

"But our teacher was Lenin, our Great Leader!" quipped Anatoli Yakovlevich, playing his high ace. "And he, as you know, spoke Russian!"

"He also spoke German and Swedish and French. They say he knew six languages altogether. And you find it difficult to learn just Georgian," I advanced, remembering that the best defence is attack, at the same time continuing to execrate myself for falling for that provocation and getting drawn into a senseless skirmish.

But my card was weak against his hand. Sensing this, he got more and more heated.

"The fact is, Lenin was a genius! And his native language is Russian! So everyone should be taught Russian," declared Anatoli Yakovlevich, already celebrating victory.

"So let's speak German, so as not to offend anyone," I replied, feeling as if my heart was about to jump out of my chest.

"Why's that?" Anatoli Yakovlevich asked, peering at me with a malicious sneer.

"Why? Because Marx spoke German! And Engels too! And they, if you please, were Lenin's teachers," I launched my shot at him with sarcasm, sure that with this utterance I had finally managed to end our foolish dispute with a good thick full stop.

Anatoli Yakovlevich was confused and did not know how to reply. I was silent for a while, awaiting a retort, but my neighbour, surprise surprise! was silent, crushed by the weight of my response. Then I smiled with self-satisfaction and winked at Bezhan, as if to say "We got him, eh? On both shoulders!" Bezhan smiled gratefully in reply.

Satisfied with the silence of my crushed opponent, I demonstratively closed my eyes, as if to say "that's all, the dispute is over." I just lay there, eyes closed, until I felt that a relative calm had been established in the ward, broken only by the shuffle of the slippers of the neighbours leaving for the dining room for supper. I waited wearily for the door to open and some mummy to bring me my helping – something remotely resembling the shape of a *kotleta* on the now hateful pearl barley, with a miserly splash of a grey mass here for some reason honoured with the name of sauce. All this munificence would be crowned with a piece of tasteless bread, albeit from a real loaf, of the same grey colour. The pudding would be either *kissel* without sugar with a film floating on the top, or a glass of pale, cold tea. I was not in the least mistaken about the menu, but I never guessed the server. Mary brought me my supper!

"This is for you!" she said, smiling from the doorway. And she raised the tray up high, leaning over the plate, and sniffed and really screwed up her eyes, expressing bliss. "M-m-m, yum-yum, it smells delicious! They must have finished the starch, and now they just have to feed us on real meat *kotlety*!"

"Put it on the bedside table, please, and I'll eat it later," I said.

"No, no, immediately!" she urged me. "It'll only do you good if it's hot!"

I looked at Mary in surprise and with concern. Her gaiety seemed put on – what inner strength of spirit do you need to look carefree and hide your true feelings after being categorically refused an operation?

"But have you had supper?" I asked.

"Yes, a light one. Mind you, from tomorrow I will be living off the best!"

"Why's that?" My heart ached unpleasantly at the thought that Mary would be discharged, and I would be left here on my own, with no-one to brighten my loneliness.

"I'm being sent to the Institute's sanatorium for a cure. It's nearby," she added. "Here, in the Moscow area, in Peredelkino. The electric trains run from the Kiev Station. I will be able to come here from time to time."

I was speechless, but as I looked at Mary she quickly glanced at the door and rewarded me with a quick, light kiss.

"But do you know why they are sending me there?"

"No."

"To fortify me before the operation! That's what they told my parents. Are you glad?"

"What do you think?"

"I know you!" Mary gave me that bright surprising smile, which I have dreamt of ever since…

On the morning of the next day Mary left for Peredelkino. For the first time I got up on my own and actually saw her to the exit.

The farewell was brief and sad. Not very confident that she would be able to come and see me, I still asked her to. After her departure the days in hospital crept by tediously, as if Mary had taken the light with her. Only then did I really feel that I was in hospital with sick people around me…

The rotteds' ward became even more crowded and stuffy, and the long monotonous conversations Anatoli Yakovlevich had with his wife, who visited him every day, were simply driving me mad. I could no longer stand seeing them looking at each other tenderly for hours, hearing her with a strict mummy's voice demanding of her spouse a detailed answer: what and how much he had eaten that day, what fluids he had drunk and in what quantity (she, like the doctors, called any drink a fluid). I was forced to hear reports even of the number of times he had been to the bathroom.

The tedium was becoming intolerable. It was driving me out of the ward – get out! quick! So I had started being forced to get up, and would sit for hours in the foyer on a sofa, talking about anything to anyone, so long as I did not return to my ward while my neighbour was billing and cooing there with his big better half. I usually preferred it if Anatoli Yakovlevich was tired by the time of my return, so he was not capable of imposing a dispute which turned out to be interesting to him alone and no-one else in the ward. Our nocturnal youth get-togethers for a while saved me and Dima senior not only from Anatoli Yakovlevich's unnecessary disputes, but from his brutish snore. That snore was a veritable trial for us, one could even say a torment to which he inquisitorially condemned us, apparently for our incorrect – from his viewpoint – attitude to life… No tongue has the art to describe these tortures any other way. It was an inhumane snore. I could only drop off by reaching a point of desperation and subsequent complete indifference to everything on earth. But even worn out by forced insomnia I slept as if on a tank track, like a tractor driver with his rumbling, rattling old crock.

Our get-togethers were good, but could have been better still, were we not importuned by solicitous heart patient mummies. Vitya

(Vitalik from Ward Six) quickly recovered after the operation, and his mother was insanely glad of that. The fragile little woman importuned with great insistence. She would spend whole days scurrying between ward and kitchen, as if not hearing Vitali's ceaseless reproaches that she was irritating him.

"Fine, fine!" Alexandra Matveyevna would say, and immediately withdraw obediently, running to the kitchen for a short while, but only to come back in a few minutes and ask:

"Vit, darling, would you like fried potatoes, eh? Shall I bring them?"

"Mum, you and your potatoes! There's no respite from you!" Vitali would rebuke her, madly happy that finally all the anxieties and terrors concerning the operation were behind him.

"Alright, alright, don't take offence, darling!" Alexandra Matveyevna would reassure him, backing towards the door without taking her eyes off her son. "But if you grow hungry, just say the word, don't be shy!"

"She won't let us have a chat!" Vitya would grumble. "Are you going at last? The guys want to chat, but you keep interrupting!"

Alexandra Matveyevna hastened back to the kitchen to expend the care unclaimed by her dear son on the dirty dishes which the young mummies had forgotten in their talk, or had perhaps left unwashed on purpose, so Vitya's mother had something to occupy herself with.

Our get-togethers were especially successful when Rita was on night duty. After bedtime, everyone capable of walking would secretly troop to the staff physician's office for a fun time, jokes and a laugh. Those whose operation was still to come would greedily listen to us veterans. But they preferred not to remember those who had been refused an operation, so as not to darken the mood.

Not only was Mary refused an operation, but also Lena and Valentina. Lena, for example, immediately discharged herself, and went home with a light heart. Perhaps she was even glad it had turned out that way. She was getting married, there were pre-wedding arrangements to be made, the girl was confident nothing could get in the way of her happiness. I even got the impression her crooked front teeth gave Lena far more grief than a heart defect which she was reminded of only by doctors' conversations and the ohs and ahs of her corpulent, tearful mother. Valentina was another matter – she was absolutely grief-stricken, although one could say they refused her at her own wish. Valentina required a guarantee of the doctors, which surprised every one of them no little. For they had, quite the opposite, been requiring a statement saying we were going for the operation voluntarily, aware of the risk and that we might die. This statement untied the hands of the surgeons, entitling them to experiment. But Valentina insisted, and as a result they refused her. It proved impossible to convince Valya that it was not the fault of the doctors, but of her disagreement with the existing regulations.

"But why should I run the risk?" she said to Lida, when the latter appealed to her to see reason and sign the statement. "For whose sake? I have no-one except my sister. For her sake, what? She loves me now, but if I die – will her love last long? She'll cry for a week or two and forget. She has a husband, children, a job. You're a different case, they're waiting for you at home, you have someone to run a risk for. You're all like that, I'm just me..." Thus would this grown-up woman with childish sincerity weep for her unlucky fate, she wept bitterly and pitiably, and then for the umpteenth time she would say that they who were to have the operation were the luckiest people on earth – even luckier than those who had already had the operation.

"So, go for the operation!" said Lida, who had been operated on just a week before. "Who told you you would die?"

"Why should they say it? I see it in their eyes! Why do you think they want to operate on me? I'm single, childless, they can take a risk on me. But I'd rather die just so than under the knife. I'll live a little longer and then pine away like an unpicked flower..."

I was surprised that Valentina, a woman who looked all of forty, should compare herself to a flower, moreover unpicked... She wept inconsolably, lovingly stroking her thick, beautiful, long hair. The crown of healthy hair on the head of the seriously ill Valentina was an object of the envy of many women.

Puny and quick as a crow, Lida tried to console her:

"Don't bury yourself yet! Even without an operation you'll live another hundred years!"

"No, Lidochka, I shan't live long!" howled Valentina. "It's you who will now live a hundred years!"

"Yea, yea..." drawled Lida pensively and sighed. "Now it does look as if I'll live, unless that mother-in-law of mine drives me to an early grave – the meanie!"

Serafim, our new boy, found this conversation boring, and got up to go. The guys were worried: if Fima was not with them – his mother, Mila Mikhaylovna, would turf us out. She started working with us the day after her Serafim was accepted at the Institute, and not as a nurse's aide or a cleaner, like the other mummies but, albeit temporarily, as a nurse, according to her qualifications. At first we did not take her seriously, although, with her eternally worried face and very important look, she would sweep along the corridors like someone possessed, in her light blue gown, like the most 'genuine' nurse. But we had underestimated her. In a matter of days, before our very eyes, she became a highly important figure at the Institute, and she was fully in control of our floor. However crafty Babka Nastya was, we were clever enough to outwit her, and besides, she was old and it was hard for her to chase us. Mila was another matter. Moreover, sooner or later Babka Nastya would go home, and Fima's mummy never went out and was with us inseparably.

It would have been 'anything goes' for us, were it not for the zeal with which Mila Mikhaylovna fought for our strict observance of the routine. Soon she became the terror of our nocturnal get-togethers. Wherever we hid, however quietly we sat, even in the dark, without light – she would unfailingly seek us out and create a grandiose scandal. Our sole salvation was Fimka, her eleven-year-old son, supercilious beyond his age. While he was with us, Mila Mikhaylovna would not touch us, and seeing Fima get up and making to leave us, we would each try to stop him:

"Serafim, where are you going?" Vitali asked in a pitiable voice.

"Stay, we're going to tell jokes now!" added Slavik, who was having the operation next day. He naturally wanted to be with his friends a bit longer.

"No, no…" replied Serafim slowly. "Your jokes are somehow not funny. I've heard enough for today."

"Wait, Fima, sit down! I'm just going to tell an interesting story," said Rita, whose authority Fimka regarded more highly than ours – she was a nurse, after all.

"No, I'm off!" he replied, and without hurrying, with dignity, just like a grown-up, he walked out of the staff physician's office and firmly shut the door behind him.

But in an instant the door was flung open and on the threshold appeared she whom we had been 'waiting' for.

"Bedtime!" our strict controller announced.

"Mila Mikhaylovna, but we've only just got together. You must know tomorrow Slavik has his operation!" Vitya implored.

"This is not a holiday camp, it's a hospital."

"Exactly, it's no holiday camp."

"Vitya, don't answer back! I'll tell your mother!"

"But did I answer back?"

"What do you think?"

"Mila Mikhaylovna, just five minutes. After all, Slavik's operation…"

"Nazarli, I thought you were cleverer."

"You thought correctly."

"No! It's a pity but I seem to be mistaken. Sorry."

"Is it worth grieving over? A piffling difference: not cleverer but not stupider either…"

"Nazarli, you remember what you promised your physician?"

"No, I've forgotten."

"Then I'll get them to remind you tomorrow!"

Everyone knew this was not an empty threat, and Mila Mikhaylovna would definitely tell.

Rita stood up.

"Anyway, guys! Mila Mikhaylovna is right, go to bed. Slavik has the operation tomorrow, he needs to rest, to have a good sleep."

"Rita!"

"Don't quarrel, guys! We'll talk later."

"When's later?"

"Vitya! What's up, can't you see?"

"It's always like that. People just get together, and someone's bound to turn up – someone with nothing better to do than spoil other people's fun!"

Mila Mikhaylovna puffed like a monitor lizard and left, having achieved her objective – everyone had dispersed to their wards.

I only saw Slava three days later, visiting him in the previous ward, where he had been taken back after the operation.

"Everything's OK!" he smiled, when I shook his feeble hand. "How are you?"

"Just the same! The cosmetic suture, curse it, won't heal!"

"I say, did they take Fimka for the operation? Somehow I didn't see him next to me in intensive care," said Slava.

"No, they didn't take him… they sent him to the Paediatric Institute."

"Like Mary?"

"No, Mary's in the sanatorium. They simply postponed the operation, as it turned out."

"I know," Slavik responded in a very feeble voice.

"Fine, you rest. Lida will tell us later. She has some news."

And the news was shattering. In the evening of that day, when Slavik had had his operation, Lida whispered conspiratorially:

"Guys, they're not accepting Fimka for an operation at all! But you… the main thing…" Lida blinked her dark little eyes frequently. "See Mila doesn't get to know anything. They say things didn't work out between her and the doctors… Anyway, she intruded into some relationships…"

"Explain yourself!" Dima senior couldn't wait.

"But no-one must hear! If they learn that it was me…"

"Fine, Lidochka, we understand – we're all true heart people… Don't be afraid!" implored Vitali.

"Well, it's like this…" Lida fidgeted on her seat and looked anxiously at the door. "In short, they told me… Well, anyway, she found herself in the centre of some sort-out between Institute personnel… something about taking a lover – and it all got out of hand!"

"Mila did not take kindly[4] to that!" drawled Vitya theatrically.

"Quiet you!" Dima senior interrupted him. "Or we'll all catch it…"

"In short," Lida summed up, "It seems she didn't just want to boss us, obviously we were not enough for her."

"Now, you're going too far, Lida!" exclaimed Vitya. "And where is Fimka in all this?"

Lida became nervous.

"Well, I don't really know… I'm telling you what they told me. In brief, Fimka is being sent to the Paediatric Institute. They probably want to treat him, as he has bruising…"

But Serafim never came back to us from the Paediatric Institute. The poor boy died, lasting till only a few days before the operation.

---

4 Translator's note: Mila means "kind" in English.

                AK WELSAPAR

After his death we saw Mila Mikhaylovna for the last time, when, collecting her son's belongings, she sobbed bitterly. Weeping, grief-stricken, we witnessed her only once, and till then she seemed to all of us just a stone idol, a piece of flint not subordinate to human feelings.

"I'll sue the lot!" she cried hysterically in the corridor. "They will answer to me for everything. For everything! The law is on my side! Bandits! They killed my boy!"

Having wept and threatened her due, Mila Mikhaylovna gathered Fima's things and left, and no-one ever saw her at the Institute again.

MARY

Mary kept her promise and came to see me three times from Peredelkino. And at the beginning of November she returned from the sanatorium for good. She looked devilishly attractive and fresh – the rest had done her good. She had not put on weight, she had even got a little thinner, but her eyes radiated with some extraordinary inner light, making her face still more comely and her mood was elated and excitable.

On the very first evening Mary helped me wash my hair, and she gained some experience of this, as she did it on each of her visits. In two months my curls had grown so, they formed an impenetrable thicket on my head. The washing took place as follows: I stood, leaning over the bath, and held my chest, where under the bandages my heart beat hurriedly and joyfully, while Mary soaped and disentangled my hair. When this procedure was finished, I felt so much better in myself, that I immediately enfolded Mary in embraces. But to lock ourselves in the bathroom was an unheard-of impertinence, as was to stay too long, also. We needed at any cost to find a cosy nook, and gathering up my daring and cheek, I went to Olga (my) Nikanorovna to ask for the key to the changing room. She may not have even believed my fabrications, but she still gave me the key, as if testing for strength my relationship with Mary which had not yet been consolidated completely. Here it was – the key to happiness!

Mary and I met downstairs in the changing room, not long before bedtime. With my right hand I embraced my beloved, and with my left I held tight the damned bandage, lest my furiously beating heart should accidentally fall on the concrete floor, but, I swear! – never, either before or after that tryst have I embraced so tightly even with two hands. Mary's lips burned mine…

After that unusual, so wished-for tryst, when everyone was quiet, we stole to our floor, displaying the utmost caution, stepping

　　　　　　　　　　　　　　　AK WELSAPAR

on tiptoe. I waited for the door to close behind Mary, who skipped noiselessly into her ward, and I wearily made for my bed. I fell asleep immediately, and that night even Anatoli Yakovlevich's wild snoring did not prevent me from falling into a deep slumber.

Before breakfast my unquiet neighbour kept trying to grill me on where I had disappeared to all evening.

"I went for a walk," I replied evasively. "In the street."

"You wouldn't be walking in the street for long now – it's cold. Here, if you'll excuse me, it's not your Turkmenia." Anatoli Yakovlevich looked me in the eye quite good-naturedly. "And I don't seem to have seen Mary. Did you by any chance go for a walk the two of you?"

"There you go! She was probably in her ward."

"She wasn't in the ward," Anatoli Yakovlevich smiled, revealing his big rabbit teeth. "The women already know everything…"

"But then they're women!" I responded sharply in the hope that he would finally leave me alone. "It's not fitting to quote their secret knowledge…"

From further interrogation I was rescued, one could say, by a pure coincidence…

"That infection!" exclaimed Anatoli Yakovlevich unexpectedly, carefully sinking onto his pillow. "Did you hear it? Squelch, squelch, it just won't tighten up. And now it's so deep, it seems to go right to the heart… Have I got to go around all my life with that whistling?"

"It'll probably pass," I responded lazily, deep down delighted that the speaker had found another subject of conversation; I was hoping that his health was much more interesting than, for example, my light-hearted – from his point of view – Institute adventures.

"No," said Anatoli Yakovlevich, "not everything passes of its own accord. And a man has to take care of his own health himself. My wife will bring me some *mumiyo* today. It comes from Ustyurt. If you drink two tablespoons morning and evening, in two weeks any break will knit. And a cleft – surely that too… It's for non-knitting of bones."

"Yes, *mumiyo* is a good remedy."

"If you like, Manya will bring you some too. Just a gram is six or eight roubles. And two grams will be enough for you!"

"Fine."

"But to buy it for real and her bring it back, you realize…"

"Consider that I've already bought it."

Here Mary looked into our ward and lit it up with her morning smile.

"Hi, Nazarli! Yulia Alexandrovna has come to see you."

"I'm coming!"

Yulia Alexandrovna was waiting for me by the entrance, wrapped in a brown knitted scarf so only her eyes were visible.

"It's so cold today!" she exclaimed as soon as she saw me. "I don't mind the frost, but it's windy too. Just as well the Good Lord prompted me to wrap up well. I've been at it since morning – your father sent a small parcel. There are some pomegranates to cheer you up. There's a letter, too. And the other day they rang up. They asked if you were alright here. And they're alright, thank God…"

"Aunt Yul, lend me sixteen roubles, if you can."

"What do you want to buy?"

"*Mumiyo*."

"No need. They've sent you some *mumiyo*. It's in a little cellophane packet. And they've written saying how to dilute it. And I've brought some honey, as father said it'll be rather bitter without honey. And there's milk, already boiled, but drink it while it's fresh, and keep the flask closed to keep in the heat."

"Aunt Yulia, I still need the money. I've already ordered it, it's awkward to refuse it now."

Aunt Yulia looked at me with that gentle smile.

"As you will. Fine, I'll bring it tomorrow. But put the little smoked sausage in the fridge. And don't eat it without bread, without bread it won't fill you up. Write home to say what's happening and how you are. Father's worried, asking when is my dear son being discharged?"

"Aunt Yulia, thank you very much. I'll go now."

We said goodbye and I hastened to the hall where, of a Sunday, all our guys would meet, and others too. At the matinées, as we called these meetings, we all told one joke each. I got there as Anatoli Yakovlevich was speaking.

"…so he says give me a Pepsi-Cola! So they give him one. He drinks one bottle, another one – nothing. He sits there and thinks maybe it's not enough. He drinks some more – nothing. So he has a couple more. Not a thing! Here we go, he says, we've got the fucking pep but we're no damned cooler!" Anatoli Yakovlevich gave a deafening guffaw.

Someone sniggered. I saw Mary look down in embarrassment, then I caught Lida's wily, sardonic smirk.

"May we laugh now?" asked Vitya.

"You may," allowed Anatoli Yakovlevich condescendingly.

"But where?"

"Where there's no damn cola!" exclaimed my neighbour, his cackle once more deafening us listeners, bored with a hoary old tale that was totally unfunny.

I went to the ward and for an unbearably long time waited for Mary, but she never came, although she had promised to. We only met in the evening, as we had agreed, in the changing room. Our secret meetings had become a ritual, I lived by them alone. I was indifferent to everything under the sun, I had forgotten who I was and where I was. I think all the stitches had been pulled out, my chest was healing; and the daily dressings morning and evening, although painful, had long become habitual. Then they started doing them every other day and Suzanna Temirovna cheered me up, saying at this rate it would soon be possible to "lay on the ointment" and that's as good as final recovery.

Several more days passed like that. Mary and I often went to the notice board in the hope of finding her surname there too. At the end of the following week, at last, they put up the long-awaited time-table of planned operations, and, like a school-leaver accepted for a college, my beloved girl with undisguised jubilation said to me:

"Look, there it is, there's my surname!"

And, in fact, it was the first to catch my eye.

"Only it's number thirteen, unlucky…" whispered Mary, smiling wanly only at my promise to hold a feast with champagne for her sixteenth or seventeenth – as soon as she returned from resuscitation.

"We'll certainly have a booze-up," I reassured her. "But you'll have to lick your wounds, you'll still be such a feeble little thing, I won't even be allowed to kiss you."

"But suppose I give you a kiss in advance, here and now?"

"Won't you be afraid of anyone?" I nudged Mary, who was intoxicated with joy, and then reasoned: "No, let's go to my place! There's no-one in our ward now – the guys are with their friends, and Anatoli Yakovlevich is seeing his wife off."

Taking advantage of a precious minute, in broad daylight we threw a hitherto unheard-of feast in our poky ward – a feast of sweet kissing!

It was unearthly passion, albeit extremely careful, quiet and innocent. It was on that day that Mary showed me how passionate she could be in the whirlpool of happiness.

"Till this evening," I said, squeezing her dear little hand with tenderness.

In the evening, as soon as Babka Nastya had gone home, Mary and I met in the changing room. Olga (my) Nikanorovna this time gave me the key with great reluctance and warned:

"Only don't you guys fall asleep there. As it is, someone has already noticed. Just as well it's one of your own…"

"We won't fall asleep, I swear," I exclaimed.

"Well…" Olga (my) Nikanorovna smiled distrustfully.

"Mary, my dearest," I said, as soon as we had locked ourselves in the changing room, "be a sweetie, and don't dare even think anything bad of me!"

"Fine," she promised.

I embraced her by her slender waist, found in the darkness her half-childish lips – hot and quivering…

"And give me your word that you will not be afraid. And that you will obey me always and in everything!" I whispered in a voice breaking with excitement, when our lips had separated.

"Simply obey you!" she burst out laughing light-heartedly in her little silver voice, forgetting for a second that we were in the changing room with precarious rights.

"Fine," I unwillingly agreed. "Only in what I asked you about."

"And what did you ask me about?" she asked me teasingly, and ran her fingers through my curls. "You'll have to wash your own hair now. I'm not likely to be able to."

"But you may recover very quickly – look at Lida, for example…"
Mary would not let me finish.

"You try and wait for me, delay discharge, till I return from resuscitation, alright?" she asked.

"I'll try," I replied encouragingly. "The bones seem to have joined, but the tissue is slow to heal."

"But is the *mumiyo* helping?" asked Mary and, barely touching, she ran her finger along the edge of the gauze bandage. After a while, she added: "You're doing well, you're recovering, I can feel…" She laid her hands on my shoulders, and her fingers lightly tickled my neck, behind the ears. I was involuntarily transfixed, awaiting a fresh helping of untold tenderness, and we were borne to a transcendental height, where there was no knowledge of the troubles and sorrows which seemed to recede far, far away from us in our close embrace.

We remembered Mary's coming operation only the following morning – on an extraordinarily sorrowful day in our life within the walls of the Institute of Cardiovascular Surgery. The day was darkened by the news of the cancellation of the operation. I hastened to see Mary, very worried about her condition. She was seated on the bed, head cast down, and did not even pay me any attention, so profound was her tragedy. I squatted before the girl, looked carefully into her eyes, not knowing where to begin… I was in total confusion, the news had engulfed us like an avalanche. We were crushed. At that moment all words seemed superfluous, and my attempts to talk to Mary were fruitless. Only once did she respond dejectedly (but it would have been better if my ears had not heard):

"I don't want to live like this… To die slowly, day by day, knowing that even hope has died. In a few years I will be all blue… It's terrible!"

I was in shock, in a stupor from the sense of what she had said and her tone. And no less dejectedly I forced myself to speak:

"Now, please… don't despair!" I implored. "What if your heart is inverted? The Americans do operations even on those, so they will soon be done in our country too!"

But Mary looked at me wearily and pitiably. I went cold from her look of resignation. I realized that words were now meaningless, for they had lost their magic. If there was any way of consoling Mary, it was no longer with words. It was a pity we were not alone in the ward, I could not embrace and protect the girl, and the only thing I ventured was to lightly touch her hand in parting.

"Till this evening!" I whispered, leaving with a heavy heart. In the doorway I looked round, Mary did not look back at me.

But in the evening…

"Mary! Mary!" I heard the frenzied cry of the little girl who had recently joined the department. She had spent days on end following close behind Mary.

I ran out of the ward and saw the little girl was already surrounded by the women – all of them were at her side; and the duty doctor and nurse, both with blanched faces, white as a cinema screen.

"The car! Mary!" the child mumbled incoherently between sobs. No-one could understand anything. The duty doctor was going to run somewhere one moment, only to come back after a few steps in the hope of finding out what was going on. They brought some water in a mug and made the girl drink a few draughts. "Over there... Ambulance," she whispered, waving her hand in the direction of the avenue. The nurse grasped the girl by the hand and took her to the procedure office.

The duty doctor ran downstairs, and we followed. In the avenue, right by the curb, was an ambulance, along with several police cars. Two people in police uniforms were measuring with a tape measure the skid marks of the car which had run Mary down, and a man in uniform was questioning eyewitnesses, quickly noting down their evidence on his pad. Now and again the darkness was illuminated by a photo flash. It was all like some banal film. I could not believe that Mary was its heroine. It was impossible to believe it. The doctor beckoned us out of the cold and told us to return to the Institute, but no-one would come away – his words were dissolved in the murmur of the crowd and the hum of the street, the noise of the avenue, which did not abate but was only narrowed down to the place where the police cars had blocked off several lanes of traffic.

Forgetting about everything on earth, I pushed my way through the crowd to the driver of the little old Moskvich, an elderly man who was weeping and repeating at the same time:

"She didn't throw herself under my car! Not under mine! It was a black limousine – they rush like madmen, the scoundrels. I was behind. I didn't even see her, I swear!"

I listened to his oaths and wept with him. I do not remember how I managed to fight my way through so close to that driver, but I found myself between him and the policemen, who were questioning him. I looked at the driver through my tears, and the policemen stared at me in bewilderment, as if they could not make out who was this young man – dishevelled, coatless, grief-stricken. And why was he weeping so bitterly...

But I was not interested in them, I kept listening to the rambling story of the driver of the Moskvich, fearing to miss a single word.

"It's not my fault!" he continued. "I swear it's not my fault! She pushed the little girl away and ran. But they, you know yourselves how they race. He swept past, and she was right in front of me. Those kind don't give a damn about brakes! It's not my fault, I swear! I'm hardly… Oh, just my luck!"

Mary passed away three days later in the "first aid" hospital, without ever regaining consciousness. Now no-one will ever know why she acted in this way. It seems incomprehensible, but it happened… Mary herself finished writing the page in the book of her life, she herself placed the full stop.

"Stupid girl!" said Anatoli Yakovlevich, picking the cherries out of a jar of fruit salad. "Contrary Mary! She knows no moderation. What sort of people are you? So, for you it's all or nothing. Who needs that? Well, she threw herself under a car, what's the most harm she has done anyone? What did she prove to anyone? Marry a fellow, at last, live like a human being, and then, as they say, God rakes you to Himself…" He spat the stones into his fist. "Dying, Nazarli, is something we all manage to do!"

I turned my back on him and on his words, so as not to see or hear anyone. Convulsively seizing myself by my quaking shoulders, I sobbed to myself, not wishing to share my grief with anyone, and not wishing anyone to see my burning tears.

Thus did my Mary so absurdly snap off her life…

MEETING WITH DESTINY

I was awoken at night by some kind of mechanical tapping. It was as if an alarm clock was ticking resonantly right next to me. In my sleep I had got cramp in my muscles, my arms lay like feeble bonds along my body, I needed air and there was an overpowering stinking stuffiness in the ward. Overcoming the now usual pain in my chest, I raised myself on my elbows and looked at Bezhan. He was asleep, lying on his back, and every second his mouth would open wide in hopeless attempts to catch just a mouthful of oxygen from that stuffy air, just a tiny mouthful, so necessary to him after the operation, already the third in his not so long life. Even in the darkness it was evident how he was suffering. I did not immediately realize that in the ward there was something unusual, something unsettling and alarming. Finally, I reckoned what was the matter: Anatoli Yakovlevich was not snoring as he always did. He was lying on the pillows, arms spread freely apart, and I thought my neighbour was sleeping the sleep of death, and I myself was afraid when I thought that. I was seized by some animal fear; half-awake, I could not immediately determine the source of the danger, from where it was threatening, but I felt it was quite close by, next to me. The nocturnal quiet of the ward and corridor was violated by clear measured beats, like the clicks of a metronome. I listened closely – where was this sound coming from?

Behind the wall, in the women's ward, someone started crying, but apparently while asleep, because the crying stopped just as suddenly as it had begun, and a profound silence reigned once more. My hope, that this shrill female crying would awaken someone nearby, was not fulfilled. No-one woke up; anyway, in hospital crying – in the night or the day – is a normal thing.

Meanwhile, the stark tapping of the metronome rang out ever louder, with a growing stubborn persistence, and I even imagined that the air bore the burning smell of engine oil lubricating the searing hot pinions of a clockwork mechanism. I made desperate attempts to reach the 'reins', but they slipped aside somewhere and I was not yet able to raise myself without them. I groaned, clutching at my chest, which had suddenly started to ache, but the sound of my groaning painfully stuck in my parched larynx. And the metronome beat louder and louder. Sweating like a pig, I finally reached the gauze 'reins' and sat up with their aid. And only then did I realize that it was certainly not a metronome tapping.

This was how Anatoli Yakovlevich's heart worked… "Tuk… tuk… tuk… tuk…" it counted in time with the breathing of his broad chest. With surprise and some relief, I looked at my neighbour. Oh, God… Is that how his heart goes? Can a human heart really emit such sounds? I felt something unnatural, something wrong. It could only be that in his chest there beat and gnashed something hitherto unknown to me – a mechanical motor!

In the nocturnal silence this mysterious mechanism worked violently, loud, filling all the surrounding space, the whole world with its endless "tak… tak… tak… tak…" I was slightly surprised that I had not heard this tapping earlier, before tonight, although we had for some time been lying next to each other in the same ward. Had I really been so self-absorbed as to not hear this tapping? Then I reckoned that previously there simply had not been the possibility of discerning it: during the day, even in the quiet hour, on this floor there was more than enough noise, and at night apparently Anatoli Yakovlevich artificially 'disguised himself' by thunderously snoring so that the walls of the ward shook. But today he had for some reason run out of vigilance, and behold, I had discovered his secret: next to me lay not a person but a robot! A self-confident, non-doubting biorobot, whose main programme was survival, was not to understand the actions of a representative of that feeble, mercurial biological species ignorant of moderation in her maximalism. Mary, from the biorobot's viewpoint, belonged to that type of people who in time must inevitably yield their place under the sun and living space to other creatures – strong, decisive, purposeful, full of the thirst to live and prevail.

The time of the biorobots has not yet come, but it certainly will, and the mechanism beating in Anatoli Yakovlevich's chest is already counting down its approach.

At that moment my neighbour slightly opened his eyes, and I shuddered at the sudden thought that he might have been watching me for a long time and knew what I was thinking then... I was horrified, you could say I was even cowed.

I wanted to get up, to call someone for help, to tell the duty doctor everything, but I was so enfeebled from stress that I could not even stir. With a quiet groan, I lay back on my pillow. Maybe it was this soft groaning that awakened some monitoring instrument concealed in Anatoli Yakovlevich's skull, and my neighbour immediately started to snore in his usual deafening, booming way...

Later, in my post-operation life, I again occasionally met such humanoid beings with mechanical hearts. Externally, they were not in the least different from people, only their eyes, if you looked carefully, would radiate the cold lifeless light which I first noticed in the eyes of Anatoli Yakovlevich. Now, on encountering such a glassy look, piercing and indifferent, even if there is noise all around, I immediately hear the familiar tapping. It is not always the same: "tik-tak, tik-tak, tik-tak, tik-tak!" – thus do some mechanical hearts hurriedly register; others tap more measuredly: "tak... tak... tak..." And some beat with menace: "tak-tak! Tak-tak!" just like Anatoli Yakovlevich's heart. At such moments I want to run point-blank – anything to get away! It's just not safe for an ordinary person to be next to a biorobot. Incidentally, they cannot even be compared to ordinary robots. After all, the latter are not meant to do people any harm – unless they are terminators from horror films!

...At the beginning of winter, on a frosty December day, with a bundle of my meagre hospital chattels under my arm, I found myself outside the gates of the Institute of Cardiovascular Surgery. Next to me was Yulia Alexandrovna, Aunt Yulia.

Saying farewell to us, Suzanna Temirovna examined the X-rays and could not conceal her surprise.

"Look, it's incredible!" she exclaimed. "Who could have thought he would leave us in less than half a year?"

I just smiled at her, firmly convinced that it was not just the medication and the dressings which had performed that miracle; not just the *mumiyo* which I took in secret from the doctors, not the ruby-red juice of the sweet Karakala pomegranates... And not even the art of the surgeons. I had saved my own self from death by my inexhaustible desire to live! I had protected the little flame of my immortal soul from the cold whiff of non-existence.

But the next moment, walking through the snow-covered gardens along the narrow winter path leading to the large, busy avenue, I was already prepared to admit the absolutely indisputable role played in my recovery by the surgeons' prowess, the multi-coloured bitter tablets and even the most ordinary, daily, routine dressings which became for long days and weeks part of my sad hospital way of life. But I would admit this only to laud to the skies the magical strength of earthly love in my miraculous resurrection!

I was suddenly possessed by a profound world weariness, with every feeble step agonizing – why was it not darling Mary escorting me, but why not she? Why had I not now by my side her who, without knowing it herself, gave me such strength, when it was so needed?

"Careful… Careful, my dear!" Aunt Yulia prompted me at almost every step, tightly wrapped in her winter shawl, as she walked with me through the frozen winter gardens, worrying simultaneously about me and herself, evidently understanding quite well that she hardly had the strength to help if – God forbid! – anything should happen to me on the narrow, icy path. We walked one behind the other slowly and with difficulty.

My heart was trying to strike each beat, gradually flooding its heavy weariness with the sweet moments of a still fragile life… And I realised what a warm and tender love I was destined henceforth to keep in my heart both in winter chill and summer heat.

We succeeded in safely mastering the short, but dangerously slippery, icy pavement and reached Lenin Avenue and halted in a state of indecision. The way out to the zebra crossing was cumbered with high snow drifts bespattered with muck from under the wheels of passing cars. I shuddered involuntarily: we were quite near the place where Mary recently stood before her fateful decision. It was here that she stepped to meet destiny, her Destiny.

My heart ached sorely – I imagined her having just made her desperate, tragic choice between life and death, pushing her little companion away from the road, and running to meet the long black limousine. But it arrogantly and cruelly abused her: it would not let her die instantly under its wheels, yielding that dubious honour of becoming an involuntary murderer to a feeble old Moskvich.

The biting cold hanging in the air nipped my ears painfully. My rabbit fur hat hardly fitted onto my shock of three months' growth of hair and protected neither my forehead nor the back of my head in the least. My light Polish jacket, bought on the cheap several years before, back in my student years, was obviously not intended for the harsh Russian cold. We had to wait a long time. The one-legged traffic lights guarding the pedestrian crossing stood forlornly on the curb, buried under a drift of dirty snow, but the colourful stream of cars flowed continuously past us, paying no attention to the red eye of the iron crock. I was gulping the cold air like an endless ribbon of ice, and the air was breaking through into my lungs, which for the past weeks had been unused to the freshness of the street and seemed to leave in my bronchi a fluffy trail of frost. I was slowly mutating into a block of ice: my hands were numb, my feet were no longer mine. The chill wind easily penetrated the fabric of my coat, reaching my chest and painfully nipping the tender young skin of the wound. This made me huddle and hunch myself under the gusts of wind. Hastening finally to return once more to the now half-forgotten healthy life, my heart thumped in great alarm for its future and mine. We were separated from the new life by an endless flow of cars, which kept us on the kerb and would not let us go forward. My heart was just striving to break out of my chest, disgruntled that the file of cars would not pay attention to us people.

"Why are you exposing your chest? You'll freeze! Hunch up a bit!" Aunt Yulia was urging me, helplessly looking along the length of the avenue in the hope of seeing the last car in the endless stream of iron horses, even standing on tiptoe for this purpose. But she craned her neck in vain: there was no end in sight to this ribbon, this heat-breathing iron serpent. "Just our luck to get here in the rush hour! Oh, it's no good – now it'll be like this everywhere! But hunch up a bit! You'll get a chill on your wound and then you'll be in trouble. Who was to know that you came here in just a jacket? An overcoat should have been sought… Keep out of the wind, dearest," she wailed pitifully.

Ahead, beyond the highway, was the free, healthy life, and behind my back towered the Institute, and I stood between them, like a lost soul. I took a rather deep gulp of air which made me cough, and I remembered that I was not yet completely healthy, and that today's discharge was a pure formality, and my obsessive, relentless fantasies of the last few days and weeks, which had pursued me while asleep and awake, were still just a sweet, longed-for dream.

I stood in the cold, in the wind. Next to me was Aunt Yulia, wrapped up for winter in a hundred scarves, so she could not turn her head. Like a *matrioshka* doll, she had to turn her whole body whenever she wanted to talk to me. Neither my father nor my brother were in Moscow now. Father had not managed to fly in for the discharge, and brother had immediately after the operation flown faraway to the Urals to continue his studies. So, as it turned out, no-one was meeting me and I was certainly not being accompanied by her...

On both sides of the avenue many people had gathered at the crossing, and all were waiting, agitated, and the most impatient tried to cross in short dashes, doing one lane at a time, but each time they were turned back ashore by the piercing whistle of the policeman standing in his stall – his 'starlings' glass nest' not far from the traffic lights. I was one of those improbably hastening; my heart was now beating furiously, and at times its unaccustomed galloping was painful and frightening. At that minute the bustling street was for me an insurmountable barrier between institutional life and the real life which I was eagerly striving for. But I was perforce halted right at the beginning of my journey; the cars crept and crept from East to West and from West to East, and there was no end of them in sight. I was now exhausted with waiting. My loyal companion, tender-hearted Aunt Yulia, incapable of changing anything, was also tired and waited submissively, drawing her head into her shoulders.

On the other side of the avenue I saw the frosted hoarding of the Baykal shop, where in the autumn I had often bought Fanta and Pepsi. To the right of it stretched the Podarki gift shop, to the left towered the Akademicheskaya Hotel. All this for some reason strangely excited my heart, which, although repaired, was still weak. I was returning to life, it was surging in me and before me, but it was quite unfriendly to me, as if it was hastening to remind me of its laws, of the traps and restrictions planted all around. With growing alarm and excitement I looked at the unending stream of cars bespattered with dirt from the road and the eye of the traffic lights staring at me, out of superstition appearing to me as a malevolent sign, an evil omen. It was very raw and fraught. I remembered the guys who could not return to life; and here was I, standing face-to-face with life. I did not know whom to pity more – those departed or myself surviving the lethal Marathon? I wanted to cry, but my eyes stayed dry, and my wounded heart hung in my breast like a cold stone. Some time would elapse before I could thaw out my soul among my family, and really mourn those hospital friends who had been by my side but would nevermore return to our insane life. I would cry like an insulted, disillusioned child. Anyway, all that would happen later, but meanwhile I was standing here, on the avenue, stiff with cold, endlessly swallowing the invisible, dry tears, storing them in myself, in order a few months later to sob and weep them out, mentally returning to the difficult days of my life.

"Look, there's a girl waving at you!" said Aunt Yulia, turning to me, and her glance indicated the opposite side of the avenue.

I peered and saw – from the other shore Olga (my) Nikanorovna was waving at me, smiling broadly, showing her big white teeth. I waved back at her, mouthing a guilty kiss. She responded by barely noticeably shaking her head, something I was already acquainted with. At that moment I felt how penetratingly my soul was accepting Olga's feelings…

At length, the frozen whistle of the good policeman made the brakes screech and the multi-lane stream of cars seemed to hit an invisible barrier and was stilled for a time. The people rushed towards each other: women, men, sexless children wrapped up for winter; some in twos, some on their own, carrying parcels, bags and 'diplomat' cases. In the very middle of the avenue, on the police island, I hurriedly embraced Olga (my) Nikanorovna, and said farewell to her. Forever. And, merging with the crowd, went to meet my destiny, which had already tested me for strength, making me go through so much grief at the very beginning of my journey!

Soon I was densely surrounded by bustling, snowy, frosty Moscow, in which I wanted to dissolve myself without residue, forgetting about everything. But I did not know how to rid myself of the burden of the last dramatic days, weeks and months which had accumulated in my soul. In a search for passing happiness I began thirstily catching people's glances, and in them everything could be found: gladness, sorrow, indifference and tenderness… I walked towards people with an open heart. My glance fluttered among other people's eyes, like a melliferous bee among flowers, as if gathering the life-giving elixir of hope… And I was sincerely glad if suddenly someone coming towards me should respond, if only for a moment, if only they would let me into their heart. And I became stronger. Every step still cost me an effort, but even walking became easier, for I was finding myself again, drinking in with relish the long-awaited bustle. With every step, with every moment I was fired up by one thing: the thought that I had come back to life. I had conquered death, and everything else was unimportant.

The world, my world was being bathed in white snow, gaining its primordial purity and innocence. Bewitchingly, the big snowflakes were slowly floating from heaven, bestowing love on all and everything. The most blessed snowflakes were for an instant delayed on girls' long eyelashes, there to melt, to dissolve into eternity, warmed by girlish hot breathing…

The Tale of Aypi

by Ak Welsapar

The Tale of Aypi follows the fate of a group of Turkmen fishermen dwelling on the coast of the Caspian Sea. The fear of losing their ancestral home looms over the entire village. This injustice is being made to look like a voluntary initiative on the part of the fishermen themselves, whilst the ruling powers cynically attempt to confiscate their land. One brave fisherman from the village rises up to confront them and fights for his native shore, as a response to an act of cruelty inflicted on a defenceless young woman centuries ago. This unjustly executed soul returns as a ghost during this troubled time to exact a terrible revenge on the men of the village.

The relationships among the characters mirror the eternal opposition between the forces of nature, with the intervention of mystical forces ratcheting up the tension.

Buy it > www.glagoslav.com

Death of the Snake Catcher

by Ak Welsapar

This book features people from one of the most closed countries of today's world, where the passage of time resembles the passage of a caravan through the waterless desert. This world has been recreated by a true-born son of that mysterious country, a Turkmen who, at the will of fate, has now been living for a quarter of a century in snowy Scandinavia. Is that not why two different worlds come together in *Ryazan horseradish and Tula gingerbread*, to come apart in *Love in Lilac*, in which a student from the non-free world falls in love with a girl from the West?

In the story *Death of the Snake Catcher*, an old snake catcher meets one on one with a giant cobra in the heart of the desert. In the dialogue between them the author unveils the age-old interdependence of Man and untamed nature, where the fear and mistrust of the strong and the hopes and apprehensions of the weak change places but co-exist as ever. *Egyptian night of fear*, in which a boy goes to an Eastern bazaar and falls into the clutches of depraved forces, is created in the writer's characteristic style of magical realism, while the novella Altynai celebrates first love, radiant and sad, pure as virgin snow.

Buy it > www.glagoslav.com

A Brown Man in Russia -
Perambulations Through A Siberian Winter
by Vijay Menon

A Brown Man in Russia describes the fantastical travels of a young, colored American traveler as he backpacks across Russia in the middle of winter via the Trans-Siberian. The book is a hybrid between the curmudgeonly travelogues of Paul Theroux and the philosophical works of Robert Pirsig. Styled in the vein of Hofstadter, the author lays out a series of absurd, but true stories followed by a deeper rumination on what they mean and why they matter. Each chapter presents a vivid anecdote from the perspective of the fumbling traveler and concludes with a deeper lesson to be gleaned. For those who recognize the discordant nature of our world in a time ripe for demagoguery and for those who want to make it better, the book is an all too welcome antidote. It explores the current global climate of despair over differences and outputs a very different message – one of hope and shared understanding. At times surreal, at times inappropriate, at times hilarious, and at times deeply human, A Brown Man in Russia is a reminder to those who feel marginalized, hopeless, or endlessly divided that harmony is achievable even in the most unlikely of places.

Buy it > www.glagoslav.com

Forefathers' Eve

by Adam Mickiewicz

Forefathers' Eve [*Dziady*] is a four-part dramatic work begun circa 1820 and completed in 1832 – with Part I published only after the poet's death, in 1860. The drama's title refers to *Dziady*, an ancient Slavic and Lithuanian feast commemorating the dead. This is the grand work of Polish literature, and it is one that elevates Mickiewicz to a position among the "great Europeans" such as Dante and Goethe.

With its Christian background of the Communion of the Saints, revenant spirits, and the interpenetration of the worlds of time and eternity, *Forefathers' Eve* speaks to men and women of all times and places. While it is a truly Polish work – Polish actors covet the role of Gustaw/Konrad in the same way that Anglophone actors covet that of Hamlet – it is one of the most universal works of literature written during the nineteenth century. It has been compared to Goethe's Faust – and rightfully so...

Buy it > www.glagoslav.com

Acropolis – The Wawel Plays
by Stanisław Wyspiański

Stanisław Wyspiański (1869-1907) achieved worldwide fame, both as a painter, and Poland's greatest dramatist of the first half of the twentieth century. *Acropolis: the Wawel Plays*, brings together four of Wyspiański's most important dramatic works in a new English translation by Charles S. Kraszewski. All of the plays centre on Wawel Hill: the legendary seat of royal and ecclesiastical power in the poet's native city, the ancient capital of Poland. In these plays, Wyspiański explores the foundational myths of his nation: that of the self-sacrificial Wanda, and the struggle between King Bolesław the Bold and Bishop Stanisław Szczepanowski. In the eponymous play which brings the cycle to an end, Wyspiański carefully considers the value of myth to a nation without political autonomy, soaring in thought into an apocalyptic vision of the future. Richly illustrated with the poet's artwork, *Acropolis: the Wawel Plays* also contains Wyspiański's architectural proposal for the renovation of Wawel Hill, and a detailed critical introduction by the translator. In its plaited presentation of *Bolesław the Bold* and *Skałka*, the translation offers, for the first time, the two plays in the unified, composite format that the poet intended, but was prevented from carrying out by his untimely death.

Buy it > www.glagoslav.com

Glagoslav Publications Catalogue

- *The Time of Women* by Elena Chizhova
- *Andrei Tarkovsky: The Collector of Dreams*
  by Layla Alexander-Garrett
- *Andrei Tarkovsky - A Life on the Cross* by Lyudmila Boyadzhieva
- *Sin* by Zakhar Prilepin
- *Hardly Ever Otherwise* by Maria Matios
- *Khatyn* by Ales Adamovich
- *The Lost Button* by Irene Rozdobudko
- *Christened with Crosses* by Eduard Kochergin
- *The Vital Needs of the Dead* by Igor Sakhnovsky
- *The Sarabande of Sara's Band* by Larysa Denysenko
- *A Poet and Bin Laden* by Hamid Ismailov
- *Watching The Russians (Dutch Edition)* by Maria Konyukova
- *Kobzar* by Taras Shevchenko
- *The Stone Bridge* by Alexander Terekhov
- *Moryak* by Lee Mandel
- *King Stakh's Wild Hunt* by Uladzimir Karatkevich
- *The Hawks of Peace* by Dmitry Rogozin
- *Harlequin's Costume* by Leonid Yuzefovich
- *Depeche Mode* by Serhii Zhadan
- *The Grand Slam and other stories (Dutch Edition)*
  by Leonid Andreev
- *METRO 2033 (Dutch Edition)* by Dmitry Glukhovsky
- *METRO 2034 (Dutch Edition)* by Dmitry Glukhovsky
- *A Russian Story* by Eugenia Kononenko
- *Herstories, An Anthology of New Ukrainian Women Prose Writers*
- *The Battle of the Sexes Russian Style* by Nadezhda Ptushkina
- *A Book Without Photographs* by Sergey Shargunov
- *Down Among The Fishes* by Natalka Babina
- *disUNITY* by Anatoly Kudryavitsky
- *Sankya* by Zakhar Prilepin
- *Wolf Messing* by Tatiana Lungin
- *Good Stalin* by Victor Erofeyev
- *Solar Plexus* by Rustam Ibragimbekov

- *Don't Call me a Victim!* by Dina Yafasova
- *Poetin (Dutch Edition)* by Chris Hutchins and Alexander Korobko
- *A History of Belarus* by Lubov Bazan
- *Children's Fashion of the Russian Empire* by Alexander Vasiliev
- *Empire of Corruption - The Russian National Pastime* by Vladimir Soloviev
- *Heroes of the 90s - People and Money. The Modern History of Russian Capitalism*
- *Fifty Highlights from the Russian Literature (Dutch Edition)* by Maarten Tengbergen
- *Bajesvolk (Dutch Edition)* by Mikhail Khodorkovsky
- *Tsarina Alexandra's Diary (Dutch Edition)*
- *Myths about Russia* by Vladimir Medinskiy
- *Boris Yeltsin - The Decade that Shook the World* by Boris Minaev
- *A Man Of Change - A study of the political life of Boris Yeltsin*
- *Sberbank - The Rebirth of Russia's Financial Giant* by Evgeny Karasyuk
- *To Get Ukraine* by Oleksandr Shyshko
- *Asystole* by Oleg Pavlov
- *Gnedich* by Maria Rybakova
- *Marina Tsvetaeva - The Essential Poetry*
- *Multiple Personalities* by Tatyana Shcherbina
- *The Investigator* by Margarita Khemlin
- *The Exile* by Zinaida Tulub
- *Leo Tolstoy – Flight from paradise* by Pavel Basinsky
- *Moscow in the 1930* by Natalia Gromova
- *Laurus (Dutch edition)* by Evgenij Vodolazkin
- *Prisoner* by Anna Nemzer
- *The Crime of Chernobyl - The Nuclear Goulag* by Wladimir Tchertkoff
- *Alpine Ballad* by Vasil Bykau
- *The Complete Correspondence of Hryhory Skovoroda*
- *The Tale of Aypi* by Ak Welsapar

- *Selected Poems* by Lydia Grigorieva
- *The Fantastic Worlds of Yuri Vynnychuk*
- *The Garden of Divine Songs and Collected Poetry of Hryhory Skovoroda*
- *Adventures in the Slavic Kitchen: A Book of Essays with Recipes*
- *Seven Signs of the Lion* by Michael M. Naydan
- *Forefathers' Eve* by Adam Mickiewicz
- *One-Two* by Igor Eliseev
- *Girls, be Good* by Bojan Babić
- *Time of the Octopus* by Anatoly Kucherena
- *The Grand Harmony* by Bohdan Ihor Antonych
- *The Selected Lyric Poetry Of Maksym Rylsky*
- *The Shining Light* by Galymkair Mutanov
- *The Frontier: 28 Contemporary Ukrainian Poets - An Anthology*
- *Acropolis - The Wawel Plays* by Stanisław Wyspiański
- *Contours of the City* by Attyla Mohylny
- *Conversations Before Silence: The Selected Poetry of Oles Ilchenko*
- *The Secret History of my Sojourn in Russia* by Jaroslav HašekCharles S. Kraszewski
- *Mirror Sand - An Anthology of Russian Short Poems in English Translation* (A Bilingual Edition)
- *Maybe We're Leaving* by Jan Balaban
- *Death of the Snake Catcher* by Ak WelsaparRichard Govett
- *A Brown Man in Russia - Perambulations Through A Siberian Winter* by Vijay Menon
- *Hard Times* by Ostap Vyshnia
- *The Flying Dutchman* by Anatoly Kudryavitsky
- *Nikolai Gumilev's Africa* by Nikolai Gumilev
- *Combustions* by Srđan Srdić
- *The Sonnets* by Adam Mickiewicz
- *Duel* by Borys Antonenko-Davydovych
- *Zinnober's Poppets* by Elena Chizhova
- *The Hemingway Game* by Evgeni Grishkovets
- *The Nuremberg Trials* by Alexander Zvyagintsev
- *Soghomon Tehlirian Memories - The Assassination of Talaat*
- *Mikhail Bulgakov - The Life and Times* by Marietta Chudakova

More coming soon...

www.ingramcontent.com/pod-product-compliance
Lightning Source LLC
Chambersburg PA
CBHW032038180726
48284CB00008B/2645